The Wedding Cake Girl

For Laura,
best kid in the universe

Author's Note

To create the Santa Rita Island of this book, I started with the beautiful Santa Catalina Island, off the coast of Los Angeles, and made as many changes as I needed to (and there were a lot) to tell my story. Santa Rita is therefore a fictional island, as different from the real Catalina as it is similar. All of the book's characters are from my imagination (especially the disagreeable ones) and any similarity to a real person is accidental.

My thanks to one real person, Ron Moore, of Dive Catalina, who patiently answered my many questions about scuba diving. Thanks, too, to the crew of the Scuba Cat, who gave me a tour of their vessel, a real live working dive boat.

If, despite the expert help I've received, any errors have crept into this book, they are mine alone.

Finally, although my character, Alexandra, is dying to take off and explore the world, she will always love and come back to her island home. And Catalina will always have a special place in my heart.

Thanks and happy reading!

Anne Pfeffer

The Wedding Cake Girl

Anne Pfeffer

Chapter One

Mom stands at the kitchen counter in her pink apron that says "Sue's Wedding Cakery, Santa Margarita Island." She's experimenting with a new frosting. The kitchen smells like a bank of fresh wild mint growing along a stream.

On my good days, I think of Mom as "The Caked Crusader," whose mission in life is to fill the world with perfect wedding cakes. On my bad days, I think more like my friend Zack who, after we saw the film Titanic, began calling Mom "The Iceberg."

"Why?" I had asked him.

"Because she's in your way."

He didn't have to remind me what happened to the Titanic.

I have to talk to her now. I've gotten special permission to attend an advanced oceanography class this summer at Beach City College, which is awesome, because I'm just a senior in high school. Or will be in September.

But the deadline to enroll is in three hours, at five o'clock. And Mom doesn't know that. The $1700 tuition is due immediately upon acceptance, and she doesn't know that either. In fact, Mom doesn't even know this class exists. Every time I go to talk to her about it, I end up putting it off.

Like now.

I need to bring in the rest of the supplies, which I've just picked up at the freight barge. I run out to our van, parked in front of our house, and open the back. With its painted pink wedding cakes and its "Sue's Wedding Cakery" lettering, no one's ever going steal this vehicle. Even it weren't almost fifteen years old.

Sweat trickling down my neck, I tie my long coppery hair up into a knot. I yank on the biggest box, filled with bags of flour, and get it up in the air, my knees almost buckling beneath me.

"I got it, Alex."

It's Zack. My diving partner and best friend since I was six. He lifts the box from my hands and jerks his head toward a smaller one. "Take that."

I blink. Whatever happened to my old friend, the skinny kid with the stick legs and pencil arms? This new guy has sun-streaked hair, broad shoulders, and strong, muscled arms that make my heart swoon.

His Uncle Dizzy's old pickup truck, which Zack borrows whenever he can, is parked at the curb. "I was driving by and saw you, so I stopped to help."

I pull myself together. "Hey, I'm on top of this one!"

He grins down at me from his still surprising new height of six feet. "Yeah, yeah," he teases me. "You've proved how strong you are. Now chill and take the other box."

We dodge garbage cans as we walk down the path that runs along the side of my house to the back patio. Zack's in front, which allows me to observe the excellent way his pants fit him. I sigh. Too bad he's with Rosie now.

"What did Sue say?" Zack asks. "About the Beach City thing?"

"I haven't told her yet." My toes curl in my sneakers as I consider this minor detail.

Zack and I drop our boxes outside the kitchen door and walk back toward the street.

"Why don't you just wait until next year and apply to some really good schools?" he says. "You don't care about Beach City College."

10

"It's the only place I can go, Zack."

He stops short on the path, making me bump into him from behind. Butterflies explode in my stomach as I leap back from him, my face turning hot.

"Alex, you can go anywhere you want," he says, "—on scholarship, too. You're the perfect candidate: way smart and dead broke."

"The point is, I need something close by. I can't leave Mom completely on her own." Beach City College is an hour away, door to door. I could go there full-time, but still come back on weekends to help Mom.

"Sue's got you so wrapped around her finger. Let her manage for herself."

We've had this argument a million times before. I appreciate that Zack cares, but he just doesn't get how much Mom needs me. And no way am I going to be like that so-called man known as my father, who abandoned her. And me.

We arrive at our parked cars.

"So I'll see you at the Point then?" I say. "For our dive?" I picture us hanging out in one of our favorite underwater spots, where the fish practically know us.

Before he can answer, a curtain of glossy black hair swings out of the cab window of his truck. It's her—Rosie Martinez. I grit my teeth. It's not that I don't like Rosie. It's just that, when she could have had any boy on the island—why did she have to take the one who's always been mine?

"Zack?" Rosie says. She and I exchange cool nods.

"I'll just be a second, okay?" Zack says.

Her head disappears.

Zack shifts his weight and looks away, turning red. "I'll drop her off and meet you at the Point."

I watch him drive away, then, like a prisoner to the guillotine, go in to face my mother.

You'd think she'd want me to get a college education, but that would mean me leaving Santa Margarita Island, which we all call Santa Rita. It's basically the tip of a volcano that reaches higher than the water around it—a sharp, rocky set of crags and cliffs poking up out of the Pacific Ocean. The few humans on it live on the tiny strips of flat land along the island's coast.

Since we only have one town—Paradise, population 3,121—and a bunch of resorts, most people who live here escape regularly to shop, travel, and otherwise check out the rest of the planet.

Those people aren't the daughter of Sue Marshall. For her, those twenty-two miles of ocean between Los Angeles and Santa Rita might as well be a million. She almost never leaves the island, so neither do I.

I am so ready for a change. A big one.

As I enter the kitchen, Mom's voice screeches to me. "Alexandra! My God!"

I know a maternal meltdown when I hear one. "What is it?"

She thrusts out a sticky note with the name "Samuels" on it. Barefoot, with her small features and wide-spaced hazel eyes, she looks like a lost kid. Her voice quavers. "I just found this under the stove. It must have fallen off the refrigerator."

"Yeah, so?"

"The Samuels cake! We need it for tomorrow. And we're totally out of ingredients!"

I force myself to speak gently. "Mom, I made the layers for that cake on Monday. I'll take them out of the freezer in a couple of hours."

"How....?"

"You know I keep all the orders in the computer." A headache begins. It's our little secret that, despite all the cakes we sell, we're hanging on by a fingernail, reeling from one crisis to the next and barely covering our expenses. And that, although Mom puts in her time, much of the hard work is done by little old me.

"If you'd just let me, I'll show you my spreadsheets. They work really well." Anything would work better than Mom's medieval system of sticky notes on the refrigerator.

Not answering me, she pours herself a glass of iced tea and sinks into a chair at our little table. She crosses her thin legs, swinging one foot, her strawberry-blond hair fluffed like cotton candy.

"I have an opportunity," I say. Quickly, before she can work herself up again, I tell her about the oceanography class. "When Roy asked them, they made a special exception to let me in." Roy is my high school science teacher.

"It'll give me the background to do an awesome research project next year."

"If you let me borrow the oven money for the tuition, I'll get a second job this summer and pay you back." I know Mom has some money saved up for a new oven. The one we have now is an ancient commercial model that Mom bought and installed when I was little.

Mom studies her hands. "It was only $800. And it's spent." She avoids my eyes.

"Oh." I can almost taste my disappointment. It figures that the little bit of cash we had is gone, probably to fund her habits of take-out food, mani/pedis, and impulse mail order purchases.

My inner bulldog springs to life. "If I can get the money somewhere else, can I do it?"

Mom's face sets into hard lines. "We're swamped in the summer, and you want to work an extra job? *And* go away for three weeks?"

"I'll come home every weekend."

Her expression closes down. "It doesn't seem like such a good idea."

Tears of frustration spring to my eyes. "You know this would be great for me!"

"And *you* know we've promised our clients their cakes! You can't spoil a person's wedding day."

"But it's okay to ruin my life!" I bolt from the clean kitchen. My mother following, I pass through the dining room, which we've equipped with a portable work station and keep immaculate for baking, and into the living room, where the scenery changes.

Here, where we spend free time and take our meals, the upholstery flaunts its stains and smudges. Dust lives undisturbed on every shelf, while last night's takeout dinner still lies in cartons on the coffee table.

We would never dream of making a cake in such a grubby room. As I storm toward the front door, I think bitterly that we treat our cakes better than we treat ourselves.

Chapter Two

"Alexandra, don't run off like that!"

"Zack's waiting for me. We're going diving."

I bring my air tank from the garage and swing it into the back of the van beside the rest of my dive equipment. "I have to be at Sky Point in fifteen minutes," I say, slamming shut the van's back doors. I want to drive off and never come back.

"It's so dangerous. A diver got trapped in an underwater cave the other day. And they couldn't get him out in time." Mom's jaw is set so tight I can see a muscle jump in her cheek.

"I'll be careful." I pull away in the van. My knuckles whiten from gripping the steering wheel, while a sour feeling oozes through my belly.

Maybe Zack's Aunt Jenna and Uncle Dizzy can lend me the money. I'll call them tonight. I glance at my watch. I have to send my response to Beach City now, before we dive.

I head for the Point, focused on the road, waving occasionally to people but not stopping to talk. The only person I want to see right now is Zack. I try to loosen my hands on the steering wheel, but they clench on, no matter what I do.

I thought mothers were supposed to be there for you, not grind you down. I jerk the steering wheel too hard, then have to readjust as I turn out onto Beachfront Road and accelerate to pass a couple of slow-moving golf carts. Due to Paradise's narrow streets, they're what most people on the island drive. Only business owners are allowed permits for full-size cars.

As I barrel the van into a parking space at Sky Point, my eyes scan the shoreline and water, checking the currents and wind conditions. Zack'll be here any minute.

Instead, my cell rings.

"I gotta problem. Rosie and I have to go to her aunt's house." Zack's voice sounds about as unhappy as I feel.

"This came up now? In the last hour?" My eyes burn, and I wish I had my sunglasses.

"Yeah, Rosie kinda sprang it on me."

I'll bet she did.

"But I've been thinking we should dive Squatter's Cove on Sunday," he says, sounding apologetic.

"Okay." It's not like I have a choice about it.

"I'm really sorry, Alex. I'll call you." He hangs up, leaving me standing there ready to chew nails.

I have an hour until the deadline to respond. Using my cell, I log on to the Beach City College website and find my application.

Two boxes. *Yes, I will attend. No, I will not attend.* If I say no, my plan's already dead at step one. If I say yes, I've got to find $1700 immediately. Is that even possible?

A pelican swoops down and lands a few feet away from me. It's clearly one of the bold ones who hang around the pier begging scraps off the fishermen. He inspects me in a hopeful way, standing tall enough for his head to reach past my knees.

"What should I do?" I ask him. He inclines his head, as if he's carefully considering my question. "Sorry, no fish." He clacks his beak and glides away on huge wings.

I watch him go, my thoughts circling along with him. I can't abandon Mom, even though I think about it every single day. You can't fault people for what they think, right? It's what they do that matters. I'm not my father. I'm *not.*

16

I can do this. I'll find some money to borrow. Taking a deep breath, I scroll down to "yes" and hit the button. The minute I've done it I think *omigod*. I can't do this. How'll I ever get the money? My head still aches and my insides boil. I take another deep breath and look to a row of ridiculously tall, spindly palm trees, their spiky fronds outlined against the sky. The palms are motionless, which means no wind. And good diving.

The water's calling to me. But I should go home. *Never dive alone.* It's the first safety rule of diving, even for someone experienced, like me.

I'm used to being good little Alexandra, who always follows the rules, gets the job done, does the right thing. Mom'll go apecrackers if she finds out I went down by myself.

But she doesn't have to find out.

I open the back doors of the van and begin to pull on my wet suit with angry little yanks. It's a warm day. Almost immediately, I can feel myself sweating inside the neoprene suit. I buckle my weight belt and grab my tank and fins. A few minutes later I'm ready and standing on the edge of the dock.

With or without Zack, and whether my mother likes it or not. I'm going diving.

Chapter Three

I take a giant stride off the dock and drop into the ocean. The cool green water closes over my head and calms me as I drift for a second or two. Under water, my tank now feels light on my back, my wet suit no longer sticky and hot.

The slow and steady *whoosh, whoosh* of my breathing through the regulator fills my ears as vertical streams of bubbles run up to the surface. I like to imagine my fears and problems floating up too, rising away from me and disappearing into the air. But this teensy issue of the Beach City class, which I've now told them I'll attend even though Mom has said no, does not disappear so easily. I focus on encapsulating the problem into a bubble, and then herd it with my eyes upward and out of sight.

In front of me stands a kelp forest. Rooted in the ocean floor, the huge stalks with their long, rippling leaves rise up through the water, hundreds of them, forming a massive tangled canopy at the top.

Instinctively, I double check for my diving knife, a large, blunt-tipped one that I love because Zack gave it to me. I always wear it strapped to the inside of my right calf. Playing it safe, I decide to stay in water only thirty feet deep, in a nice open area where nothing bad can happen to me.

I nod a greeting to a garibaldi who floats by, his fins undulating, looking comical and fantastically orange. Then my favorite appears, a school of Pacific jack mackerel, headed in my direction. Its beauty sends a shiver through me. The hundreds of fish move and turn in exact unison, their silver bodies glimmering in the sunlight that filters down from the surface. Right, left, down and away, the fish depart as a unit, like a single giant creature.

Above me, a diver swims hard for the top. From his small frame, I'd guess he's a kid, maybe ten or twelve years old. A prickling goes over me to see the skinny legs, flailing, as he heads straight for the surface as fast as his fins will take him.

He's all alone. I wonder where his partner is.

Behind him, a heavy stand of kelp moves back and forth in the water. My mask's fogging up, so I tip it and exhale sharply through my nose. My mask now clear, I look again.

A diver's trapped in the kelp.

A big man, pear-shaped in his wet suit, tries to extricate himself, his motions rapid and jerky even under water.

A tingling rush of fear starts in my throat and spreads. Why isn't Zack here? Zack, who's even a better diver than I am, and so strong and cool under pressure. But I'm on my own.

A terrible thought invades my mind: I can leave right now and no one'll ever know. I don't want to die trying to save this man.

But I'm his only hope.

My arms and legs stiffen when I try to bend them, as if they're registering a protest. *Move,* I order them. *Now.*

I enter the kelp forest.

Slowly, I pass through the frightening fingers of the leaves. When a tendril wraps itself around my ankle, I resist the urge to yank my leg toward me, stop, and slowly back up. The kelp relaxes, releasing me.

As I approach the man, my mind races. How much air does he have left? My own supply will only last so long.

He looks up and sees me. Behind his mask, his eyes are a brilliant blue. They are focused and determined. The man raises his wrist to show me his state-of-the-art dive computer. He has only 800 psi of air left.

That's nothing. Hot terror surges through me like lava. To be on the safe side, divers normally try to end a dive with a cushion of 500 psi of air left in their tanks. This guy's practically already there.

I can tell he's ripping through what little air he has left—a big man, breathing hard from stress and fear. The sound of my own breathing speeds up in my ears, despite my efforts to keep it slow and conserve every square inch of life-sustaining air.

Knife in hand, I advance, searching around him to find what keeps him trapped. A second later, I see it. The sun glints off thin strands of fishing line nested around him. One leg's caught, and he's gesturing over his shoulder toward his tank as well. Fishing line's far more treacherous than kelp, hard to see and impossible to tear or break with your hands.

His dive computer says 700 psi of air left.

It takes only a second to slash the line around his fins, but his tank's still caught. *Stay calm.* As our eyes meet again, I push on his shoulder, hard, rotating his body, my eyes searching the dangerous tangle of kelp and fishing line behind him.

I can't see anything. My fear takes on new life, sprouting and multiplying. I can't—won't—leave him there to die.

Is that it? The sun catches a sliver of silver line, taut, as if pulled between two objects. I slip my knife in to cut it. Released, the man does a fast drift in my direction, bumping into me. I grab his arm and back us slowly away from the area where he's been entangled.

He's now down to 500 psi. The *whoosh, whoosh* sound in my ears turns fast and ragged, exactly the kind of stressed breathing that gobbles up your air supply. Breathe slowly and evenly.

We have to get out into the open fast. As I motion him to follow me, I sense a movement and realize too late that it's my knife, which slips from my fingers and plummets. Frantic, I swipe in slow-motion through the water for it, but miss. In a second, it's out of sight, erased by the kelp. I stare into the black leaves below us, willing it to come back, but it doesn't.

Zack's gift is gone. Don't think, keep going. We're still in kelp. If we hit fishing line now, we're chum.

We move forward. The closely spaced stalks force us into single file, which means I can't share my air with him until we leave the kelp bed.

We inch through the enormous tree-like kelp plants. Occasionally we stop to tear at a single leaf that has grabbed a wrist or an ankle. My mind screams at me to hurry.

Don't hurry. That's what gets people into trouble.

The kelp seems to go on and on. My heart pounds hard and fast up in my throat. We'll never get out. We'll die together, this stranger and I, caught in this forest of never-ending kelp.

Just in time, we reach an open area. Even as the man's slashing his hand across his neck, the international diver sign for "out of air," I'm handing him the alternative air source from my octopus rig—a second regulator for a friend in need. Now both of us are breathing from my tank, gripping each other's arms.

Glancing at my air gauge, I feel a sudden icy chill. I've messed up. Due to tension and fear, I've burned more than I expected.

We're going to run out of air.

We're thirty feet down. I know what I have to do. I'll give the man the rest of my air, meaning I won't be breathing on the way up. But if I don't exhale continuously as we rise, the compressed tank air in my lungs will expand and damage them, or even kill me.

I signal a stern command to the man: ascend.

Far above, a few dark lace-like strands of kelp stretch across the bright surface of the water. I reach my hand toward them, take a deep breath, and surge upward, the man beside me. I kick with my fins and exhale, ascending at a slow, controlled pace. Ignoring my lungs as they clamor for air, leaving what little bit's in the tank for him, I reach for the strands of lace, focusing on them, dimly aware of the man next to me, then suddenly feeling a strength from him as he pushes ahead the last yard, helping me upward.

Our heads burst up past the surface as we simultaneously spit out our regulators. I gasp and gulp for air, my greedy lungs raking it in with a rasping noise. The needle on my air gauge stands at empty.

The man treads water, holding my arm, his mask inches from mine. Our eyes meet, his mirroring my joy and relief. I've done it. I can't believe it. I've saved him.

What little I can see of his face confirms that he's old—grandfather age—with crazy, bushy silver eyebrows. His eyes are even more intensely blue now that they're out in the sunlight. He looks around him, shaking his head and coughing from the salt water.

"I didn't think I'd see this world again," he says in an awed tone.

Using the hoses attached to our inflatable diving vests, called BCDs, I blow some air into them, allowing us to bob on the surface of the water. We float together for a moment, side by side, still coughing and gasping and catching our breath.

"You stopped breathing," he says, after a moment.

"Emergency Ascent." I clear my throat, which throbs, feeling raw and scratchy. "We were out of air."

He shakes his head, with a look of disbelief.

We hear yelling. The boy I'd seen before waves from the far end of the long dock, nearest the ocean. I guess that he called for help, then waited for it to arrive. In the distance, a siren gets louder and louder as it draws near.

Mom. She'll sell my diving equipment, I know it. In a panic, I turn to the man. "Please don't tell anyone I was here!"

Now, for the first time, the eyes hold dismay. "But you saved my life!"

"Please? You can't believe how much trouble I'll get into."

He hesitates, then nods.

The boy on the dock removes his tank and BCD and dives into the water. He swims in our direction.

I exchange one last look with the blue-eyed man before I power away from him, easily putting distance between us with my long fins. The dock at Sky Point spans several hundred feet of the cove.

By heading for the land end of the dock, near the lot where my van's parked, I'm able to avoid the boy, coming from the other direction.

Reaching the ladder, I pull off the fins and hook the straps over my wrist, climbing up like a monkey and running along the dock with the heavy tank bumping on my back. It takes only seconds to strip off my gear and throw it in the back of the van.

I can't believe it. I've saved a man's life.

Still in my wet suit, I peel out of there, turning up onto the main road. A minute later, the town ambulance rolls by me; that's the siren I'd heard. I duck my head to hide my face as I pass the driver, Darryl. My mother dated him for a few months last year, until he decided he preferred Mona Singer, who cuts hair at the French Twist. But there's no real way to hide when you have large pink wedding cakes painted on the side of your getaway car. Every person in Paradise knows who drives that van.

It freaks me out to think that the ambulance has only just arrived. If I hadn't been there, that man would be dead by now. I shiver at the thought and drive home.

Chapter Four

I tiptoe into the kitchen, taking a read of the emotional weather. Mom's happy again—I can tell by the smell of scented candles and the harp music wafting from our CD player. In spite of myself, I feel hope stir. If I ask her a second time, maybe now she'll say yes.

"Sweetheart, is that you?" She comes into the kitchen holding two dresses on hangers. Both still have the tags on them. They're summer dresses—one a soft coral, the other a lilac floral print. Mom-clothes, soft and feminine.

"I'm trying to decide," she says, tossing her hair and holding each up for inspection. "I need to be pretty tonight!"

She heads off to her bedroom, and I follow, stopping only to grab a terry cloth robe from my room. I perch on her bed, noticing that she's lit three or four candles in here.

"They add so much atmosphere to a room!" she likes to say.

I move one that burns close to a hanging curtain, then draw the thick robe more tightly around me. She gave it to me when I couldn't go on the junior class science trip to Costa Rica. We didn't have the money. I like the robe, but would have rather gone to Costa Rica.

"So which dress for my date?" she asks.

"They're both nice." I've never understood why it takes a committee to choose a simple dress for an evening out.

"Hey! Do you want to try one of them on?" Mom's eyes are suddenly bright and hopeful.

"No!" Seeing her hurt expression, I add quickly, "I haven't washed up yet. I'll get them dirty."

"You know what I was thinking about today? How we used to make Tiny Cakes."

I mean, really. Tiny Cakes? Right now? "I remember," I find myself saying. Mom showed me how to cut small perfect cubes of leftover cake, frost them tabletop smooth, and decorate them with butter cream roses and swirls.

"And we would get all dressed up and have tea?"

"I remember." We'd put the cakes on a silver plate and serve them to my stuffed animals—a whale, a starfish, and an octopus. I remember how pretty my mother looked, holding the tray of little cakes. But after just one, I'd get full, and I didn't like cake much anyway.

"Mommy, can we go play hopscotch?" I would ask. "Or take a walk?"

"What, and end this lovely tea party?"

My thoughts go to the man in the kelp and his boy. I wonder how they're doing, picturing them telling their loved ones, seeing everyone's relief and happiness. And I'm the one, I think, a warm feeling of pride growing in my chest. I saved him. I give Mom a nervous glance. She'd go ballistic if she knew.

Always hanging over me is the fear she'll take away my equipment. I bought it used from Nate's Dive Shop on a payment plan. But because I didn't even have money for payments, Nate had let me work off my debt.

For two years, I spent an hour here, two hours there, scrubbing his floors and toilets, applying a squeegee to his picture windows, and caring for his dogs when he was off the island. I can't bear the idea that, in an instant, my mother can undo all I've done and take away the one thing I most love doing.

Now's my chance. "Mom, can we talk about this school thing again? I've got it all worked out..."

"Alexandra, I told you! We can't afford it."

I stare at her dully. "Mom, this program is exactly what I want to do." I add, "Roy recommended me for it, and they made a special exception for me."

Mom just shakes her head.

I'll go to Plan B, I tell myself. But there is no Plan B. This plan is it.

I told Beach City I'd be coming this summer. I'll have to tell them on Monday that I'm not.

I can't stand it. I'll run away.

Hearing my cell phone, I go into my own bedroom to get it. It's Zack. "You wanna hang out at Dizzy's later on?"

And now Zack wants me to be sloppy seconds. "I thought you were with Rosie and her aunt."

"Change of plans."

"Again?"

"It's been that kinda day. I'll tell you when I see you." Zack's voice rings hollowly through the receiver.

Whether I like it or not, he and I are just friends. I might as well get used to it. "Okay, I'll see you around eight thirty." I'll tell him about Mom then.

As I sign off, she appears in the doorway of my room. "Okay if I take the first shower?"

"Sure. When's Bo coming?" I heave out an exaggerated sigh.

"Oh, come on, he's not that bad!" Mom laughs, giving me a playful push.

"He *is* that bad!"

Mom's long history of poor choices in men started with my father, the weakling who deserted her when she was nineteen and pregnant.

If there were other men in the years between my dad and The Imposter, Jule Loman, I don't remember them. Jule arrived on the scene when I was eight. He was one of the captains for Santa Rita

26

Traveler, the main company that runs boats between the island and the mainland, and the only captain who had a home on the island. But he lived primarily in the nearest mainland town, Long Beach, and had business interests there.

To myself, I called him "Jule the Fool." It was the worst insult my eight-year old mind could come up with. Mom spent most of their five years together waiting for him to call or waiting for him to arrive. He doled out small bits of his time to her—usually just weekday evenings when he was on the island, and almost never weekends or holidays.

He was meticulous about remembering to send flowers for her birthday and Valentine's Day, but it wasn't until a bouquet of red roses was accidentally delivered to our house with a card saying "Happy Anniversary" that we found out he had a wife and three kids in Long Beach.

I rejoiced to have him gone, although it was hard to see my mom devastated.

Since then, Mom has only dated a handful of men, but it's as if they were all carefully selected from the ranks of known deadbeats and bottom-feeders. She took up with the latest, Bo Schwartz, about three months ago.

"You can do better, Mom," I say, although in fact, she never has.

"He has a good disposition, and he may even start getting some hours driving for Paradise Taxi. It would be a big step up for him. Financially, I mean."

"Yeah, I bet." Bo's main job is frying hot dogs and burgers part-time at The Frank 'n Flip, but he fills in with an assortment of odd jobs.

It's my mom's life, not mine, thank God. I long ago decided I'll take a different path, one that has no room in it for anything even marginally Mom-like.

In my life there'll be no guys who show up late or not at all and eventually disappear without warning, never to be heard from again. There'll be no vocationally challenged men who bum money off me and never pay it back.

I'll be smart about the kind of guys I hang with. I'll choose good ones. Like Zack. Although Rosie's gotten to him first.

"Bo's picking me up at seven thirty for a quick dinner," Mom says. "Remind me. What's on for tomorrow?"

"Two cakes," I say. "While I do Samuels in the morning, you can get Broadman organized. I'll take you up to the Inn for that, around one o'clock."

I sleep, eat, dream and weep wedding cakes. I see them when my eyes are closed and smell them even when the closest one's three blocks away. I'll never get married. Or if I do, I'll elope. Well, I'll probably have a wedding. But I'll make sure we have ice cream sundaes for dessert.

Chapter Five

After Mom finishes in the bathroom, I take a quick shower, pull on my uniform of jeans and an old t-shirt, and run a brush through my hair, which goes halfway down my back. I like it even though it's all wrong for my life of constant cake baking and scuba diving. I keep it tied back in a ponytail or braid most of the time. Tonight, I go for the braid option.

For her date, Mom has chosen the coral dress, put her hair up, and worn her pearl earrings.

"How do I look?" she asks.

"Fine." Despair surges through me at the thought of a lifetime as Mom's assistant pastry chef and style consultant.

Since Bo's not here yet, Mom walks out onto our back patio, then calls to me. "Look, there's just a fingernail of moon!" All my life she's done that, brought me out to see the moon in its different forms.

I link arms with her and we tip our faces up to the sky. The thin crescent beams out a surprisingly strong light that forms a halo around it.

"It looks like it's nestled in a bed of clouds," Mom says. "Did you know that Artemis, the Roman goddess of the moon, never married? She was never conquered by love."

Artemis was actually a Greek goddess, but I don't tell her. We gaze at the cloudy sky with its eerie light. Sometimes I think my love of nature comes from all those times I looked at the moon with my mother when I was little.

I could just leave her when I turn eighteen. But I don't want to. I need to know she'll be okay. I want her blessing.

"We'd better go in," she says, "so I can hear the doorbell." She settles herself on a kitchen chair, leafing through a magazine. "I don't want to muss my dress." She smooths it so there are no wrinkles beneath her.

Half an hour later, she's still sitting there, looking a little smaller and tired around the eyes. She freshens her lip gloss and blots it. Goes for a glass of water, then puts it aside.

I fume. What rocks does she find these guys under? "When was he supposed to be here? Seven thirty?" It's eight-fifteen by now and I have to go soon.

I remember something. "Mom, will you blow out your candles before you leave?" Then, "Never mind." I do it myself, the smell of smoke filling her little bedroom.

As I'm leaving, Bo shows up, gracing us with his presence at eight twenty-five. Mom has been standing up and stretching. She now resumes her lady-like pose seated on the kitchen chair in her dress, while here comes Bo, sure of his welcome, in an old shirt, cargo shorts, and plastic flip-flops. He has these huge sideburns and a mustache that are straight from some deservedly forgotten decade of the twentieth century.

"Hi there, stranger!" Mom says.

I glare at him. "You're late."

"*Alexandra!* Don't mind her, Bo."

I can't bear to look at them. "Bye, Mom!" I run out the door, not waiting for her reply.

Chapter Six

Someone with a whimsical imagination must have named the streets in Paradise. I head down Cinnamon Street to Carousel Avenue and turn left. It takes me all of one minute to get to Dizzy's Dive. Fishnets full of carefully preserved sea life cover the walls. Amidst the motionless crabs and swordfish, a soccer game blares from ten TVs. Brazil's playing Italy.

I squeeze my way through the tables. Zack's already sitting at the counter. Technically, since Dizzy's is a full-fledged liquor-slinging establishment, Zack and I are not allowed on the premises. But seeing as how Dizzy Malone is Zack's uncle, and Spike Malone, Zack's dad, is Chief of Police, there's no one to turn us in or arrest us. Zack and I have been hanging at Dizzy's since we were little, slugging down sodas and sitting near Dizzy at the bar, where he could keep an eye on us.

Zack listens to the person beside him, grinning broadly, his smile white against his tan. I love the way he's always himself, always calm and centered. A couple of girls walk by, checking him out, but he's waving to me.

It's okay if Zack's with Rosie, I try to convince myself. After all, I was the one who stupidly said it was better to be just friends.

Three months ago, Zack and I went mountain biking and stopped to rest on a hillside. I lay in a patch of sun with my eyes closed, while Zack walked around nearby. I heard him rustling in the grass, but didn't know what he was doing until I sat up, opened my eyes, and found him holding out a bunch of wildflowers. To me.

I leaned forward, admiring the island poppies and Arroyo lupine in his hand. "The flowers are great this spring, with all the rain we've gotten!" Then I looked up.

He had a half-embarrassed, half-determined expression on his face. "They're for you," he said.

"Oh!" In shock, I took them and sat there, looking down at them, not knowing what to say.

"I thought that maybe I should ask you out on a date. That is," he added, "if you're interested." He put on this "just-kidding" expression that masked the shy and serious Zack underneath and gave him an escape route if needed.

But the word "date" meant one thing: my mother and her men. I would never live in that world or let it touch what I had with Zack.

"I don't do dates!" The words flew out of me. I scrambled to my feet, the flowers falling from my hand. "Your friendship means too much to me."

"Yeah, I know, me too," he said, suddenly busy brushing off his shorts with angry little strokes.

"Zack, I...." I knew I'd hurt him, but I didn't know how to undo what I'd done. "Now I've dropped your flowers!" I wailed, trying to pick them up out of the long grass.

"Don't worry about it." He stalked off toward his mountain bike.

"Wait!"

"Forget it." He asked Rosie out the very next day.

I haven't been able to fix my mistake. We're still friends and diving partners, but it's not the same.

As I make my way through the tables, I'm pulled over by Darryl, the ambulance driver from this afternoon. He's sitting with Stone and Brady, two of his poker buddies. They have enough beer on the table to float a battleship.

Talking to Darryl makes me nervous. On the one hand, I want to hear about how the man in the kelp's doing. But Darryl saw me driving away from the scene, and I don't want him to put two and two together. Not that Darryl's particularly known for putting two and two together, or even one and one, for that matter, but still. I feel a stab of anxiety, realizing that now Stone and Brady will also know I was at the Point.

"Alex!" Darryl says. "Did you see anyone out on the road there by the Point? This afternoon, right before I saw you?"

I make my face look innocent. "No, why?"

"Well, it's the craziest thing. A diver saved a tourist today. He was caught in the kelp, and this diver came along and cut him out. But they can't find the diver."

"He was probably off a private boat," Brady says. "Not anyone from around here." With his wire-rimmed glasses, Brady looks like a librarian. Instead, he's a construction foreman for JayBud Builders.

"Didn't the tourist get his name?" I ask.

Darryl shakes his head. "He said he barely saw him. He said the guy cut him out of the kelp, brought him up, and took off."

"It's too bad they can't find the rescuer," Brady says. "That guy's a hero."

I'm a hero.

I feel a thrill of pride, but at the same time can't help but think, *no, I'm not.*

I leave them and go to sit on a stool next to Zack, where Jenna Malone, Dizzy's wife and Zack's aunt, subs for one of the regular bartenders. Normally, Jenna works as a server up at the Inn, which has the best pay on the island.

This is my chance to ask her about the money.

Jenna's all kindness and common sense, combined with a splash of twisted humor. She's heavy set, but what you notice are her long

33

honey hair and her violet-blue eyes. Dizzy likes to say, "Jenna's the best thing that ever happened to me."

They've never been able to have children. It's hard for me to understand a world where people like Dizzy and Jenna go without when a guy like my father easily created me, who meant nothing to him. Since Zack has a silent, undemonstrative father and a mother who died when he was six, they stepped into the parent role for him a long time ago. Even I think of them as Aunt Jenna and Uncle Dizzy.

Jenna blows me a kiss and says, "I'll bring you a Coke, honey."

"Hey, Alex," Zack says in my ear. "Sorry about this afternoon."

"It's okay." I eye him. "Why aren't you with Rosie now?" I ignore that strange little feeling of hurt I always get when I think about him and Rosie together.

"We had an argument." Zack pulls a dish of nuts toward him and downs a handful.

"Was it bad?"

He takes another handful. "She told me to go to hell."

"Oh, that *is* bad." Suddenly, I feel cheerful.

"She said I had Peter Pan syndrome." Zack scratches his head, his eyebrows drawing together.

I answer his unasked question. "Meaning she thinks you'll never grow up."

"Yeah, right." Zack snorts.

"At least she doesn't think you secretly wear green tights."

"Better not! Anyway, I never got dinner." He's crunching on pretzels now.

"I'm sorry." I try to look sorry. Rosie's always been emotional. She's appealing, I guess, if you like the spicy, high-spirited type. With big, dark eyes and a tiny waist. And big boobs.

Maybe I should think about something else. Like the fact that they might be breaking up. I feel happiness rise, like a wisp of smoke, at the possibility of having Zack to myself again.

Jenna arrives with my Coke. "Here, honey," she says to me, eyeing the empty bowls in front of Zack. "How about some burgers?"

"Awesome!" Zack grins, nodding, while I shake my head. Jenna leaves to put in the order and returns a moment later.

"I had a fight with Mom." I tell them about her reaction to the Beach City class and about the tuition, conveniently leaving out how I've already said yes. "You should have seen her today! She had this total breakdown."

Zack rolls his eyes. "Because you *let her.*"

I ignore him and pluck up my courage. "Jenna, I know this is a lot to ask...."

She listens as I tell her about my problem, her big, grave eyes fastened on me. "But what good is it to have the money if Sue won't let you take the class?"

"I'm still hoping to talk her into it."

"Sweetie, I don't know. It's a lot of money for us, and there's your mom's wishes to consider too. Let me talk to Dizzy, okay?"

Due immediately upon acceptance. Feeling lightheaded, I say, "Do you think you could maybe decide by tomorrow?"

"Sure, honey." Jenna fills some drink orders, then comes back to us. "Say, d'you guys know anything about this mystery diver? The one who saved a tourist's life?"

"Oh, yeah," Zack says to me, "did you get over to the Point today? D'you see anything?"

I shake my head. I'll tell him and Jenna the story, but not in public where people can hear me. In Paradise, a good story spreads like fire in dry brush.

I listen for a while as people sitting at the bar talk about the man who performed this wonderful feat of heroism.

"They were a hundred feet down," someone says.

"The tourist guy was almost dead when they brought him up. He had to be rushed to the hospital."

"I heard the hero saved *two* people."

They have it all blown out of proportion, but still, it would be nice if I could tell them it's me.

Chapter Seven

When my alarm clock rings at six o'clock on the morning after I saved a man's life, my mother's still sleeping off the effects of last night's date. Mom always sleeps through the alarm clock, which makes it up to me to wake her.

I pray that Jenna's talked to Dizzy about the money and that she'll give me an answer today. They're the only people I can think of who might help me.

As I shake Mom's shoulder, her head pops up from the pillow, like a turtle from its shell, except this turtle has serious bedhead and streaked mascara. She groans and grumbles at me, while I show no mercy, opening the curtains, whipping the blankets off of her, and yelling "Rise and shine! We've got two cakes today!" After yesterday, I'm in no mood to make it easy for her.

Since our fragile wedding cakes don't hold up well on Santa Rita's twisting mountain roads, we always assemble them on-site, on the day of the wedding. "After I do Samuels," I say, "I'll take you up to the Inn for the Broadman cake."

The minute I could take over for her, Mom made me her designated driver for most deliveries. She hates driving on the island's steep, curving roads.

"You might as well stay at the Inn until I'm done," my mom says. "No point in going back and forth."

"Okay," I say, tonelessly. Slave labor for slave wages, as I'll be paid nothing for a full day's work. I try to bludgeon a fly that buzzes by. "Get outta here!"

Lara Samuels has ordered a three layer cake for one hundred twenty-five guests—a dark chocolate base layer and two ascending layers of hazelnut. I check that everything I need is packed in the van—the three cake layers on their cardboard bases, round wooden dowel sticks, pastry bags pre-filled with buttercream frosting, a variety of piping heads, wax paper, spatulas, and my "Sue's Wedding Cakery" apron.

I have to go. Butter cream frosting waits for no one, especially not in June in Southern California. I head for the Channel Island Resort, a bland place with a golf course and pool.

The resort's Wedding Coordinator, Marcia, waits for me in a beige linen pantsuit, her hair tied back with a gold clip. She consults a long list on a clipboard. "I told the bride and mother you'd have the cake ready by noon," she says.

"Thanks." I get to work. Three more months. In three months, I'll be a legal adult and allowed to make my own decisions. In another year, I'll be done with high school and free to leave the island. Except for the fact that Mom can't survive without me.

Zack's right, though. She had to have managed without me when I was younger. I slam a box of piping heads down on the counter. What's her problem now?

Working fast, but carefully, I put down the bottom layer of cake, and then use all my frustrated energy to plunge short dowel sticks vertically into the center of the layer in a circle. The second layer, on its cardboard base, will rest on the ends of the dowel sticks, preventing it from sinking into and crushing the cake layer below it. I do the same with the third layer.

In my present mood, I wouldn't mind seeing a cake or two implode. I'm positively savage as I skewer the entire cake down the middle with a final single dowel stick, to keep the layers from sliding in different directions.

As I work, I daydream. Maybe the summer between high school and college, I can travel. Nepal, Thailand, the Great Barrier Reef. I picture myself diving and trekking with Zack, hanging out on pristine white foreign beaches. I know it's impossible, but I dream anyway.

To make most cakes, I copy one of Mom's designs, but Lara Samuels has requested dozens of yellow and peach butter cream roses and a blue and white butter cream sash saying "Love forever, Bruce and Lara." The cake's busy and tacky for my taste, but Lara's been very specific. I follow her orders. I've been frosting cakes since I was five and can do one like this half awake, as in fact I almost am.

As I'm finishing up, Marcia walks in with a man beside her. "Alex, this is Lester Lindstrom," she says. "His daughter's holding her wedding here in September. The first weekend after Labor Day." It crosses my mind that her wedding will fall right between Labor Day and my eighteenth birthday, which is on September 14.

Lester is medium height with pale blue eyes and brown hair that looks like it's going into early retirement. I give him points for making no effort to hide the thin spot on the top of his head—no combed over strands of hair for him.

Giving me a gap-toothed grin, he holds out his hand. I shake it, smiling. Something about this guy makes me want to smile.

"I've told him how your mother makes the best wedding cakes on the West Coast," Marcia says.

"Well, thanks! I'd be happy to help you," I tell the man.

With a polite, puzzled expression, he scans the wildly over-decorated cake I've just finished frosting.

"This happens to be the bride's design," I say, smoothly. "But we offer many of our own."

Lester gives me a sheepish look. "I'll do whatever my daughter wants. Nothing's too good for my girl on her big day."

My eyes suddenly sting. How would it feel to have a father? One who loves you and wants to give you the perfect wedding? "Here's our business card. Sue Marshall, the name on the card, is my mother."

"Thanks, Alex! We'll arrange to meet with her the next time we come out." Lester takes off.

I watch him go. Why can't Mom find someone nice and normal like him? But the good ones are always married. As if on cue, my cell rings. Mom, as usual.

"Honey, the Inn. The Broadman cake."

"Ten minutes." I hang up.

Marcia arrives with a girl and an older woman in tow. The bride and her mother. Lara Samuels gasps when she sees the cake. "It's what I always dreamed of!" she says, with tears in her eyes.

"I'm really glad," I tell her, meaning it.

Now if I can just figure out a way to make my own dreams come true.

Chapter Eight

The Santa Margarita Inn is a four star bed-and-breakfast—a beautiful old mansion on the top of Mt. Vazquez. For this wedding, my mom has told me, the Broadman family rented out the entire Inn for the weekend, plus about sixty hotel rooms in town.

"I'll bet these people think they're *all that*," Mom says. "They're actual *billionaires*—from real estate."

Mom always has plenty to say about the snobby and self-important rich, even though they're the very ones who we count on to buy our fancy, custom-made cakes. I wonder how much a wedding like this one costs. For what the Broadmans paid, I think sadly, you could probably fund an entire four-year undergraduate education. A really good one.

I put on a clean shirt and pull my hair up into a ponytail, while my mom finds a sundress, and we head off in our van. I wind my way up the mountain, each turn in the road offering a new view of the island and sea. Ordinarily, I love the drive up to the Inn, but today the sky and ocean are as flat and colorless as my mood.

We bring the supplies into the kitchen through the service entrance. Mom'll do this one alone. The high-end customers want to know she's herself attending to their cakes. After I help her put down the base and bring the cake layers in, I wander off, ready to kill some time.

After making sure the coast is clear, I walk through the French doors to see a tent and platform constructed on the lawn outside. Under the tent, round tables bear the Inn's china and silver, crystal glassware, and centerpieces of pale peach roses and white calla lilies. Those centerpieces alone probably cost more than $1700. There are place cards with names in silver-gray calligraphy and party favors in small boxes wrapped in peach and silver with a white rose on top.

It's so amazing that some people get to live this way. Some people take for granted that they'll go to college, have a good job, and be married in a beautiful place that overlooks the ocean. My parents got married at a quickie-chapel in Las Vegas. I'll be the first in my family to even attempt going to college.

A small sound makes me turn. I jump to see a guy about my own age standing a few feet away. He looks the way I imagine a young English lord would look, with a strong, angular face, jet black hair that flows back from his forehead, and an air of easy belonging about him, as if he's used to nice places and nice things. He wears a navy polo shirt with the collar turned up and khaki pants.

"I didn't hear you coming," I say, my heart pounding.

He flashes me an apologetic smile. "Sorry. I didn't mean to scare you."

A girl walks into the tent now, the same age as him, with the same black hair, cut in a china doll bob. She wears the prettiest dress I've ever seen: flowery and sleeveless with a bell-shaped skirt and a wide pink belt. I wonder why anyone who got to own a dress like that would have such a sulky pout on her face.

She stops short when she sees me, frowning. "Who are you?"

"Alex Marshall. I helped my mother deliver the wedding cake."

"Oh." The girl has heard all she needs to. "Jeremy, do you want to go into town for ice cream? A bunch of us are going, and Mom

41

said to ask you." The words come out in an impatient rush, as if she's too bored by him to even finish her sentence.

Jeremy forms his mouth into a big circle of fake surprise. "You? Eat carbs?"

"I'm taking that as a no." She turns on her heel and marches off.

Jeremy raises an eyebrow at me. "That's my sister Emma. She and I are a strange case." He pulls out two chairs from a table and sits in one, gesturing toward the other.

After a second, I sit down, trying to remember if I combed my hair. "What do you mean?"

"I mean," he says, "we are twins with no common genetic material. We have nothing in common. *Nothing.*"

Based on what I've seen of Emma, it seems like that may be a good thing.

He catches my eye and shakes his head. "Don't say it," he drawls.

I start to laugh. "You don't know what I'm thinking!"

"Oh, but I do. Because I'm thinking the same thing." Jeremy stretches his legs out in front of him, as if sprawling comes naturally to him. "So you're here for the wedding cake?"

I nod. "My mom's doing it. I just drove her up here."

"She couldn't drive herself?" He looks at me with interest.

How did we get on this subject? This isn't something I normally talk about, especially not with strangers. "She's kind of sensitive I guess." I realize as I say it how lame it sounds.

"Too sensitive to drive a car?" Jeremy makes a disbelieving face at me.

"It sounds pretty insane, doesn't it?"

"Not at all," he deadpans.

"Jeremy, dear!" An older woman pulls open the French door, waving to us. "Come see the wedding cake!"

He jumps to his feet. "That's Gram. You want to come with me?"

Feeling too shy to say anything, I follow him in. My mom stands next to a spectacular wedding cake, one of the best she's ever made. It's pure white, but somehow in the light of the dining room, it almost shimmers, looking silver. It's very simple, but elegant, its stark look softened by a trim of delicate lace at the edge of each layer. The lace is so perfect and intricate that I lean in to see it, expecting it to be real lace. But no, Mom has made it out of frosting.

"Caroline is thrilled with it," the older woman tells Jeremy. "And I must agree that it's splendid!" Caroline is the bride, I remember.

My mother looks radiant, her cheeks pink from the woman's compliment, as if she just hit the baking equivalent of a home run. Pride warms me—even if she flounders at business, nobody makes a wedding cake like she does. And I'm not too bad at it myself.

A sudden pang strikes me as I realize how rarely I see my mom looking happy. Forgetting for a moment how mad I am at her, I walk up and put an arm around her. "It's incredible, Mom."

She does a surprised double take. "Thanks, honey."

Jeremy's grandmother wears a bright green tailored skirt and jacket, with a white blouse. A simple, heavy gold chain hangs around her neck. Her face, full of laugh lines, reminds me of the apple head dolls I used to make, where I would carve a face into a fresh apple, then it let it dry into the wrinkled face of an old person.

She shakes Mom's hand. "Thank you, Sue." She turns to me. "And this is…?"

"Alex. Alexandra. Marshall." I squeak out the syllables, surprised to be noticed. Only now do I realize how tiny she is, barely reaching my shoulder.

"Hello, dear. So you assist your mother with her wedding cakes?"

"I help deliver them," I tell her. I like this woman immediately, with her warm, direct manner.

"Do you deliver cakes with your mother every day?"

"Yes. I mean, with my mother or by myself." I glance over at Mom. We don't usually let on to people how much of the work

I do. Jeremy's eyes move back and forth between the two of us, watching us with interest.

"My dear," Mrs. Broadman says, "you must be very busy this time of year. Is that your van outside?" When Mom and I nod, the older woman continues, "Sue, Alexandra... I have a request. Would Alex be willing to assist us at Caroline's wedding? We need a nice young person to carry the guest book around to guests and ask them to sign it. It will be a keepsake for Caroline and Stuart."

"We will, of course, compensate you, Alex, for your time. Are you willing to help us?"

Am I willing to work a gig at the Inn, the best employer on the island? You bet I am. Maybe this will be the first job of many. And the Broadmans will probably pay top dollar—more than minimum wage, for sure. It's all good news for the college fund.

Knowing Mom doesn't like me taking jobs from other people, I jump to answer before she can get a word in. "Oh, yes, ma'am, I'd *love* to!" I think fast. "If you give me a guest list ahead of time, I can use it to make sure I don't miss anyone." Mom flutters next to me, radiating negative energy, but I refuse to look in her direction.

"Why, aren't you clever! Of course, my dear."

"How would you like me to dress?" The thought rolls through my head that I'll see Jeremy again. And that he'll see me. I hope they won't make me wear the dorky Inn workers' uniform of black pants and a white blouse.

"I think a simple dress of your own would be fine. You'll come at five thirty?"

"Yes." My stomach rolls over from a mixture of excitement and nerves. Beside me, my mom clicks her tongue in disapproval.

After Mrs. Broadman has squeezed my hands, complimented me some more, and left for an afternoon nap, Jeremy gives me a look that I can't quite interpret. "I'll see you tonight at the wedding. Nice meeting you, Alexandra Marshall."

"Nice meeting you, Jeremy Broadman. You're the bride's... brother?"

"Cousin."

Between saving a man's life, landing a great job, this boy I've just met, and my irritated mother next to me, my head's whirling. I know Mom won't say anything here.

Sure enough, she waits until we're in the van to say, "Alexandra, why do you want to spend your time on other jobs? You've already got a job!"

The words burst out of me. "I need to earn money. For expenses."

"Your expenses are all paid." Late-afternoon sunlight puts a sparkle into the ocean on my right. My mother's profile looks stubborn against the backdrop of the shimmering water.

"I mean for some of the things I want. Like college!"

Umbrellas of every color, stripe and pattern populate the beach. Kayaks explore along the shoreline while further out, sailboats and small fishing boats dot the water.

"Why isn't anything ever good enough for you?" She draws in a ragged breath. "Why do you always have to want so much?"

I don't reply as I turn down Cinnamon Street and pull up in front of our house. Is she right? Do I expect more than I deserve? I stare straight ahead, gripping the steering wheel as a wave of queasiness rolls over me.

When Mom speaks again her voice is pleading. "Alexandra, I'd love to give you things, but every penny we make goes for basic necessities. If I gave you a wage, we couldn't make our rent payments."

"What are you going to do when… if…" I can't say it.

"When what?"

"When I … go away to college."

A heavy silence falls over us both as I pull the van into our narrow driveway. Mom doesn't answer, but instead stares straight ahead of her, as if I'm not here.

It isn't fair. The words keep going through my head. It isn't fair. "Okay, well, I have to get ready for tonight," I say as we enter our living room.

45

"Fine! Just don't think you can take the van!" She draws herself up as tall as she can and vanishes into her bedroom, closing the door behind her with a soft click.

. . .

Numb from my fight with Mom, I get ready for Caroline Broadman's wedding. I file my fingernails and toenails, smoothing off all the rough corners and even going so far as to paint them. I use clear polish so the mistakes won't show. I shower, then struggle to blow dry and brush my hair until it finally falls in a perfect curve down my back.

I iron my nicest dress, a pale blue, sleeveless linen shift. It's cheap, purchased on sale from Nancy's Dress Shack, but it fits well and looks good so long as I don't crease it by sitting down.

Now what? I should accessorize, but how? Mom would know how to put my hair up, find the right pair of shoes. Longing wells up inside me. She's just on the other side of this bedroom wall. Maybe if I went to her she would do the things that I imagine mothers do: listen to me, support me, make me feel safe and understood.

But she's in her bedroom, drifting in the ozone of her own thoughts. I think of the happiness in her eyes earlier today, how pretty she looked.

Just don't think you can take the van.

Nice try, Mom. I've already called Zack and asked him for a ride.

I decide I need some makeup. Using the tips in a magazine page I once tore out and saved, I manage a bit of smoky eyeliner, some blush, and some lip gloss. A gold locket that Jenna and Dizzy gave me and white sandals, flat ones that I can walk in easily. I take one last check in the mirror.

It'll have to do.

. . .

As usual, Zack pulls up outside my front door and honks the horn of his truck. But he jumps out and comes to greet me when he sees the new-and-improved Alexandra.

"*Wow!*" he says, a slow smile starting at the corners of his mouth and working its way across his face. It makes me warm and shivery. I love Zack's smile.

You look…." He shakes his head, as if words escape him completely. "Allow me," he says, taking a comical bow and opening the door to the cab of his pick-up. He shovels an armful of clothing, empty soda cans, and other personal debris into a plastic grocery bag, straightens a semi-clean towel that's draped across the seat, and takes my hand to help me in. His hand feels strong and rough and familiar in mine. I hate letting go of it.

While Zack guns the engine and powers us up the hill toward the Inn, I tell him about my job for the evening. He listens, turning every few seconds to look at me in a way he usually doesn't. I can feel the heat rushing up my neck and face.

"I'm calling Kap Holloway tomorrow," he says, "to find out if he's interested in me now that I'm eighteen." Kap runs the best and biggest charter dive boat operation on Santa Rita Island.

"You're calling Kap?" This is news. It's a dream job, getting paid to go out on dive boats. I always thought we'd go to work for Kap together.

"I'll ask him about you too," Zack says.

"I don't see how I could do it. I have to be available when Mom needs me, especially on weekends."

"Yeah, and that really sucks, by the way."

I glance over at him, curious at his sudden forcefulness.

He's looking at me with a sober expression. "I just want to see you get everything you deserve."

We reach the Inn, and Zack zips the truck into the unloading area near the service entrance. I don't think either of us have ever driven into the circular front driveway or walked through the main entrance.

47

Zack yanks on the parking brake. "Hold on." He jumps out of the cab, runs around to my side, and opens the door for me. He's never done that before.

"Thanks," I say to him. "Mom's being so awful. You saved me."

He smiles at me, a pure, simple open smile. Again, he holds my hand as I step down, but this time he doesn't let go of it. My heart starts thumping in my chest so hard I'm afraid I'm going to scare the birds out of the trees.

"You look beautiful." And just like that, he gathers me up in his arms and kisses me.

Feeling his lips, his hard chest against mine, I wind my arms around his neck and kiss him back, his skin warm under my hands. My mind's going in circles, but mainly I'm just feeling it, being so close to him, his breathing, his hands in my hair. It's definitely the best kiss I've ever had. Before that day on the mountain, when he asked me out for a date, I had never thought about kissing Zack or being anything more than friends with him. Since then, and especially since he started dating Rosie, I've thought about it a lot.

An alarm bell goes off in my head. Hating to do it, I push him away.

"Zack! What about Rosie?" Just because they had a fight yesterday doesn't mean they've broken up. We stare at each other. Zack seems as surprised as I am.

"I haven't talked to her since our fight." He spreads his hands, looking helpless.

I don't know what to say. It's strange to feel awkward with my closest friend.

"Call me when you're ready to leave," he says, and I nod, too confused to say more.

The Inn manager, Evelyn Armor, comes out as Zack drives away. If she saw the two of us kissing, she gives no sign of it. Evelyn knows me well, as she's been buying our wedding cakes for years. She wears a simple, but perfect plum-colored suit with a scarf held by a gold pin. Her hair, cut short, waves back in a way that softens her face. She's going over a list in her handheld.

"Hi, Alex. Mrs. Broadman told me she'd hired you for the evening." She eyes my recently ironed linen dress, which is now creased from sitting in Zack's truck. "Is that what you're planning to wear?"

"Yes, why?" I look down at myself. I look like one of those wrinkly dogs.

Evelyn taps the side of her cheek with her fingernails. "Let's see if Rebecca has something you can borrow."

I shrivel inside, thinking I would rather wear a wet suit. Evelyn's daughter, Rebecca, is in the same grade as me at Paradise High. Being forced to borrow a classmate's clothes, like some poor stepcousin, is too embarrassing to even contemplate.

We pass through the kitchen where the chef's tasting sauces and checking the progress of a large copper pot on the stove. I follow Evelyn up the stairs, still feeling Zack's lips on mine. I've only kissed a few boys up to now, the most memorable being Jose Camacho, who made out with me in a dark closet one night during a party game of Seven Minutes In Heaven.

In the dining room, I wave to Jenna, who works regular shifts at the Inn as a server. She's folding napkins with one of Rosie's sisters. Santa Rita's home to over eighty members of the Martinez family, who came from Mexico and settled on the island more than two generations ago. They own a lot of land here and Rosie's dad is on the City Council.

I wonder what kind of conversation Jenna can be having with a sister of Rosie's. Then I wonder what business Zack had kissing me. Have he and Rosie split up or not? Does he think he can mess around with me while he's still with her? He can take that idea and cram it.

Seeing me all dressed up, Jenna does an elaborate double-take, mouthing, "You look *great!*" and then, "I'll talk to you later."

"Okay," I mouth back. Tonight I'll find out if she's talked to Dizzy about the $1700. I hate asking them for it, but I'll find a way to repay them.

49

Evelyn brings me up to the fourth floor, into Rebecca's room, where her daughter's lying on her bed, a guitar beside her. I look down to hide my red face. It's bad enough having to borrow Rebecca's clothes, but having to face her while I try them on is too humiliating.

She gives a limp wave as we come in. It looks like she tried to straighten her hair again. It seems to have worked on one side of her head, but not the other. Rebecca experiments all the time, cutting and highlighting her own hair, mixing and matching her clothes in ways that sometimes work and sometimes plunge into disaster. She never seems to worry about or even notice what other people think.

Evelyn holds up a pale green silk dress that I've never seen Rebecca wear. "I bought this for you in San Francisco, remember?"

She shrugs. "I guess." I notice a new piercing, a silver stud by her eyebrow, and the remains of what looks like black lipstick.

"You've only worn it once."

"Alex can borrow it." Rebecca flops back on the bed and closes her eyes, as if the conversation has exhausted her.

I slip it on, loving the feeling of the heavy, slippery silk. Evelyn zips it up. Our eyes meet in the mirror. Evelyn nods and smiles while I gape at my reflection. A different person stands there, a girl with full curving lips and hair rippling down her back, slender and perfectly dressed.

"You wear a size 7 shoe?" Evelyn asks. "So do I." She hands me a pair of heeled sandals, which I can get by in for an evening.

I've never worn anything as beautiful as that dress, or felt so pretty. "Thank you both. These things are perfect for the wedding."

Rebecca rolls onto her side to give me a cheesy grin. "Enjoy!"

"I know you'll do a wonderful job." Evelyn smiles at me. "Mrs. Broadman's quite taken with you. She mentioned you several times to me this afternoon. Make sure you chat with her and do everything she asks you to do."

I nod, resisting the urge to smooth my damp palms along the pale green silk, then take a step forward, only to find myself wobbling in the heels Evelyn has strapped onto my feet. Just don't fall down in front of all these people, I scold myself, and head down the stairs.

Chapter Nine

"There you are, dear!" Margaret Broadman wears a long, lavender gown and, around her neck, a river of diamonds that wink and blink as she moves. "You look absolutely lovely! Let me introduce you to a few people." She takes my arm and leads me into to the living room, with its old grandfather clock, Persian rugs, and antique sofas, where family and members of the wedding party mill around.

The first person I see is Jeremy.

"Welcome back!" In his tux, his shoes shined, and his hair combed back, he looks serious and mature.

"Hi," I say, but Mrs. Broadman wants me to meet the bride, Caroline, a statuesque column of white silk with dark upswept hair and a diamond on her finger the size of a jelly bean. She's marrying a guy named Stuart Chapling, who I overhear is a Yale-educated attorney, although he looks more like a model in a toothpaste ad.

For the next hour, I move around the living room, library, and terrace with a pen and guestbook, collecting greetings. I try not to stare at the guests in their finely tailored suits and glittering evening wear. I especially love seeing the jewelry: a pendant with a huge amethyst in it, pearl and diamond drop earrings, a narrow bracelet with a row of emeralds. Watching the people move about, bright colors of their summer clothing, the sparkle of their jewels, reminds me of tropical fish suspended in the midst of coral and sea anemones.

A part of me thinks any one of those bracelets or necklaces could probably pay for the summer program at Beach City. I just want to take this one course to jump start my college education. Why does that have to be so impossible?

No matter how I feel, I can't afford to be shy and tongue-tied with these people. I have a job to do. It isn't too hard to approach a group of adults and wait for an opening in the conversation: "… saw her at Harrod's in London…," "…only water after four pm…," "…chose Stanford over Harvard…," "…the second act was dreadful…." I find these wealthy, accomplished people are happy to stop for a moment to write in the guest book.

It's a lot harder with the kids my own age. I zero in on three teenage bridesmaids chatting: "omigod, she totally starves herself…," "…. I mean, this guy in Prada's *so hot*…", "… my mom says I have to go to France with her this summer *again*…"

As if I'm not intimidated enough, I recognize one of the girls as Emma Broadman, Jeremy's unfriendly twin sister. She wears a red silk sheath that's stunning with her black hair. In my borrowed shoes, I approach, my mouth dry.

"Sure," Emma says, taking the book from me without even glancing my way. She gives no sign of remembering me from earlier this afternoon. The three girls write their messages, chatting as they do, while I stand there, invisible to them.

Jeremy appears next to me. Looking over my shoulder at the guest list in my hand, he asks, "Who's left, besides me?"

I show him some of the names still unchecked.

"You need my dad and uncle. They're over there." Jeremy points to two older versions of himself standing in tuxedos by the fireplace.

"Wow, your whole family looks alike."

"Yeah, we're practically interchangeable. Dad and my Uncle William work together with their dad, my grandfather, in the family business."

"And what about you?" I ask. Jeremy's shorter and stockier than Zack. He has a nice smile, but no guy smiles the way Zack does.

"I worked for them last summer, and it was okay, I guess. I was going to do it again this summer, but then I decided to try something completely different, have an adventure before I go off to college." Jeremy looks at me with a mildly amused expression that I'm beginning to realize is typical of him.

"Where are you going? To college, I mean."

"Stanford."

"Are you the one who chose Stanford over Harvard?"

"How d'you know that?"

"I'm psychic. And it's your turn, by the way." I hand him the book.

While he writes, I take a moment to look through a large telescope that stands in the corner. Through the scope, the town of Paradise comes into clear focus down below. Vacationers stroll along Carousel Avenue, which is pedestrian-only, getting tables for dinner and buying t-shirts and key chains in the trinket shops. The umbrellas and towels have deserted the beach, since it's early evening. One die-hard does the breaststroke all alone in an area of the harbor marked off for swimmers.

"There you go." Jeremy hands me back the book. In looping black script he has written, "Take good care of my cousin, Stuart, or I'm coming after you (just kidding). Sincerely, Jeremy Broadman."

"Thanks," I say, thinking how much easier this day has gone for me because of him.

"Do you live on this island?" he says suddenly. "I like it here." When I nod, he asks, "Is there anything I could do out here? Now, this summer?"

"Well, if you like bussing tables."

He shrugs. "Why not? Bussing tables and hitting the beach on my days off. I could get into it for a few months."

I guess anything might be interesting if you could do it exactly when and for as long as you wanted to.

"Hey," he says, "if you're from the island, maybe you've heard something about this diver? The one who saved a guy who was caught in the kelp?"

I freeze. "Why do you ask?"

"We're looking for him," he says. "The guy he saved is my grandfather."

Chapter Ten

I step back, my mouth open. "Your *grandfather?*"

Jeremy looks past me. "Here he is now."

In my mind, I see Mom piling my diving equipment into boxes and carrying it off to the dump. I look around for an escape route, but in front of me is a familiar pair of brilliant blue eyes topped by crazy, bushy silver eyebrows. The man's tuxedo is a lot more slimming than the wet suit I last saw him wearing. Margaret Broadman stands with him, beaming.

"Jeremy, darling, you're needed to help seat the guests," she says.

When Jeremy has gone, she continues, "Edward, look who I found!" She sounds delighted with herself.

Without realizing it, I've been moving away from them as they advance slowly toward me. It's only when my back bumps the bookshelves that I stop.

Edward, who is probably close to seventy, pumps my hand, his eyes twinkling at me. "It is a great pleasure to meet you again. I owe you … everything. You saved my life."

My head whirls. I've saved the life of a famous billionaire? Stunned, I try to speak, but nothing comes out.

"How did you find her?" he asks his wife.

"Well, dear, when you said it was a girl with flame-colored hair who drove a van with pink wedding cakes on it, I thought to myself—how many of those could there *be*?" Margaret tries to look modest, but then gives up. "So, I made some inquiries and learned that almost every wedding cake on the island is made by Sue Marshall and her daughter Alexandra—and delivered in a van with pink wedding cakes on it!"

Margaret takes both of my hands in hers. "I cannot begin to thank you for what you did." Her voice trembles. "Edward is my heart, my life. You are a very brave and wonderful young lady."

"Thank you," I whisper, my eyes filling with tears. If it weren't for the disaster about to occur, I would love the feeling of being appreciated and recognized for what I did.

"No one else knows. Edward and I will keep your secret," she says. "But may I ask why your identity cannot be disclosed?"

"I wasn't supposed to be diving that day. Please don't tell anyone. My mother will be so mad at me!" A small part of me feels thrilled to meet the man in the kelp, but the rest of me is entering major crisis mode.

"She wouldn't forgive you when she learned of your heroic act?"

I shake my head, saying nothing.

"Gram?" Jeremy's back. He stops short in surprise as he sees me and Margaret, teary-eyed, her hands holding mine. "We're about to start. I should take you to your seat." As he offers her a black tuxedoed elbow, he throws a look over his shoulder toward me. I don't know how I could have missed it, but his eyes are the same brilliant blue as his grandfather's. "I'll see you later, Alex?" There's a question in his voice. "After the ceremony?"

"Alexandra," Margaret says, "will you please come have dinner at our table? We would so like to chat with you."

"I'm sorry," I stammer, "but I think people would wonder if I did that." All my fears are crashing down on my head. Mom will sell my diving equipment, forbid me to ever dive again.

"Of course. Well, perhaps after dinner you will come and report to us on the status of the guest book?" The corners of her mouth hold a smile.

I have to do that much. It's part of my job. "Yes, ma'm."

. . .

The wedding ceremony's about to begin on the large veranda, where a canopy's been set up to provide shade but leave ocean views. Since the dining room's ready, the serving staff's free to watch from discreet locations. I find Jenna peering out onto the veranda from a second story window.

I put my arm through hers. "Hey," I say. I feel like I'm going to jump out of my skin. Not only is my secret coming out, but time's ticking by on the tuition money. I have to ask Jenna if she talked to Dizzy.

"Rosie's sister just gave me an earful about my flaky nephew," she says. "What's he told you about himself and Rosie?"

"Not much," I admit.

Jenna sighs. "Zack's a good boy. But he's—a boy." What's *that* supposed to mean, I wonder. Despite the fog I'm in, I tip one ear in her direction.

Jenna chooses her words carefully. "I guess things went pretty far with them. Then he tried to end it, and she didn't take it well." Lines crease her forehead. "That Rosie's strong-willed. And she's set her cap for Zack."

How far is 'pretty far'? And why did he try to end it? I wonder for a second if it had to do with me, then think no, not likely. Rosie's a catch.

From outside on the veranda, we hear the sounds of a piano and a violin. The ceremony's beginning. Jenna and I watch as the bridesmaids come down the aisle, followed by Caroline, holding calla lilies, in her sleek tube of white silk.

Now's the time to ask Jenna. "Did you talk to Dizzy?"

"Sweetie, I did. I'm so sorry—we can't spare $1700." Seeing my disappointment, she goes on quickly, "but if it would help, we can lend you $500. Could you get the rest from someone else?"

I consider her question. Her offer is a start, at least. "I don't know. I can sure try." Maybe Nate will let me work off a loan. "Thanks, Jenna!"

Stuart and Caroline start back down the aisle, now husband and wife. "Whoops! Time to get busy!" Jenna rushes off.

During dinner, between courses, I'm able to gather the last greetings I need to complete the book. As I move through the tables, I find myself wishing I could just pass a collection basket. This crowd could raise the remaining $1200 I need from their pocket change.

Pieces of my mother's incredible double lemon cake are being served. When I peek in the dining room, Margaret waves me over. She has a chair for me between her and her husband, but I hang back, glancing around nervously.

"I don't think I should sit down. Thank you, anyway."

Margaret accepts a piece of cake from a server. "You must have one, my dear."

"No, thank you," I say, although I'm starving. I nod to the server, our town librarian who also moonlights at the Inn, holding up the guest book to explain why I'm chatting with the bride's grandparents. I'm glad I didn't take Margaret's invitation to sit at the Broadman family table. If I had, half the town would know by eleven o'clock tomorrow morning.

I give the book to Margaret, saying, "It's all done."

"But this is marvelous!" exclaims Mrs. Broadman. "Edward, look at this!" She turns it toward him so he can see.

"I made sure everyone signed the book. I also suggested they write some kind of greeting or message to the bride and groom, rather than just their names." That made a difference, because the guest book's actually fun to read.

While Margaret pores over the entries, chortling, Edward looks at me appraisingly. "You seem to have mastered the fine art of delivering more than is expected," he says. "That's a rare quality. Tell me, what are you studying in school?"

"Science is my favorite subject. I want to be an oceanographer. Or a marine biologist."

The clinking of spoons against glasses interrupts us and brings everyone's attention to William, the bride's father, who's now standing, holding a cordless microphone.

"All right, everyone, it's time for a few toasts!"

"Alexandra," Margaret asks, "does Evelyn have your address so I can mail you the payment for tonight's work?"

"Yes." I whisper my thank yous to the Broadmans and slip away to stand by the doorway. Servers float in with trays of champagne flutes. The microphone travels between the best man, the maid of honor, and other speakers, then back to William. "One last toast before the dancing begins." He stands, waiting until the guests have settled down.

"There's a famous line from the great play *A Streetcar Named Desire*. 'I have always depended on the kindness of strangers.' Until this weekend, I never thought that line applied to our family. But, I've come to learn that, in fact, it does."

William stops and looks out at the guests, now very quiet. I stand there, suddenly exhausted by my warring emotions. Joy and pride from meeting the man I saved. Hope from Jenna and Dizzy's $500 loan, along with worry. Where on earth will I get another $1200? And I need it yesterday.

Jenna, having finished passing out the champagne, comes to stand next to me. I lean against her a little, and she puts an arm around me.

William continues. "I think you all know that we had a near tragedy in our family yesterday. My father was in very serious danger while scuba diving, and had a stranger not come along under the water to help him, he would probably not be with us today."

A wave of heat passes through my body. Margaret told me that only she and Edward knew.

"This person, this stranger, saved my father's life and then disappeared. No one knows who he is, and we've had no opportunity to thank him. But without him, we could not have been happy tonight. We could not have celebrated Caroline and Stuart's marriage with joy and with our whole family around us."

I stiffen and stare down at my toes, not trusting myself to look up. A few tears splash down on the plush Persian rug.

"So if everyone will please stand ...." Clothes rustle and chairs scrape back as people get to their feet.

"Let's raise our glasses to someone we've never met, a true Good Samaritan, a truly kind and brave person, who gave a priceless gift to our family through his courage and strength and selflessness. To a stranger, wherever he may be... Cheers!"

And all at the same time, a hundred glasses are raised in the air to thank and congratulate a brave, strong, selfless, faraway stranger.

Or rather, a weeping, trembling seventeen-year-old girl who's neither a stranger nor very far away at all.

Chapter Eleven

"Excuse me," I say and run from the dining room. I find a bathroom, lock the door, and huddle there for a while, too drained to do anything but sit on the toilet lid. I'm a hero, all right, hiding in the bathroom, scared of my mother. I need to leave. I do a quick check of the mirror, wash off the smeared make-up under my eyes, and head for the exit.

"There you are!" It's Jeremy, who seems to have made it his mission in life to find me wherever I am. We're under the heavy, glistening chandelier in the front entryway. Bits of light from its crystals dance on the velvet brocade wallpaper. I've never left the Inn by the front door before, but this time that's where my feet have taken me. I've completely forgotten about how I got here, or how I'm going to get home.

"Why didn't you tell me it was you? The hero?" Jeremy beams as he tries to tug me back toward the party.

"*What? I'm not!*"

"Are too. You're the stranger! You admitted it to Gram and Gramps." The sound of music and talking grows louder as Jeremy moves me toward it. "This is awesome! We are so gonna party!"

"No!" I stop so abruptly that he walks past me and has to double back. "Jeremy, you have to help me!" I grab onto the silky lapels of his tux with both hands. "My mom'll take my equipment if she finds out I was diving alone yesterday!"

"I'll speak to your mother." It's Edward. He and Margaret appear beside Jeremy's shoulder. "I'll make her understand what happened."

"She won't understand." These people can thank me and explain all they want, but they're going to leave tomorrow and go back to their world, while I'm stuck here shoveling frosting. "I appreciate your thanks so much, but please keep this secret."

"Of course we will, dear," Mrs. Broadman says. "I'm afraid I did tell William," she confesses. "I simply could not allow you to go totally unrecognized when you were right there in the room! And him just assuming the hero was a man!" Seeing my face, she adds, "But it will stay within our family. You have my word."

"Thank you. I should leave."

"I'll take you home in a golf cart," Jeremy says.

But the entry hall is filling up with Broadmans—Jeremy's father and his uncle William, their wives, a flock of cousins and now even the bride. I find myself hemmed in by smiling eyes and faces. Every single member of the family wants to thank me personally. This would be a dream come true if it weren't a total nightmare. I give Jeremy a pleading look.

"Step aside, folks. Coming through!" He grabs my arm and maneuvers me through the crowd, so we can make our escape. From the corner of my eye, I see black and white server uniforms passing by, island people gaping at me and wondering what I'm doing surrounded, paparazzi-like, by a mob of rich people, all trying to get my attention.

We almost make it to safety. We're only inches from the front door, and I'm about to breathe a heavy sigh of relief when I feel someone next to me.

It's Rebecca, holding a glass of juice from the kitchen, apparently indifferent to the fact that a fancy wedding's going on in her home. All of a sudden, she's turned chatty.

"Hey, Alex! How's that dress working out for you?"

• • •

I lurch to a stop, staring down at the ground. I can't move, can't look up, want to die or run away. Anything but face the astonished Broadman family.

"You can return it anytime," Rebecca continues, oblivious to our audience.

"I'll bring it to you tomorrow," I say in a low voice, my face flaming. I can feel my lips tremble as I study the pattern in the Inn's fancy rug.

Out of the corner of my eye, I see Evelyn pulling in like a locomotive at the station. The Inn manager takes it all in with one glance, chirps "Don't mind us!" and sweeps Rebecca up the stairs. I watch them go, keeping my eyes on the stairwell even after they've disappeared. I would do anything to vanish in a puff of smoke and never be seen or heard from again.

"You ready?" says a voice behind me. I jump at the sound of it. It's Zack, who I've forgotten to call. He has found a faded shirt that does little to hide his lean, muscled arms, and his eyes are very green against his tanned skin. He's easily the tallest—and hottest— guy in the room, but standing there next to a fleet of designer tuxedoes and evening gowns with his worn Dockers, board shorts, and long, sunstreaked hair curling out of a blue bandana, he looks like a seafaring Paul Bunyan who has wandered into a debutante ball by mistake.

A ripple goes through the Broadman family: shock from the older generation, curiosity from the ushers, and thrilled excitement from the bridesmaids. Zack bobs his head toward them, completely at ease, then, noticing Jeremy, gives him a pointed look. Jeremy drops my arm and moves away from me.

"When I called here, they said the party was ending. So I came on up," Zack tells me. "You all done?" He glances over at the Broadman clan with a pleasant expression, including them in the conversation.

63

Jeremy's face is a careful blank. Giving him a look of apology, I tell the assembled crowd, "Thank you all again so much."

I leave the Inn with Zack, while the Broadmans watch us go.

Chapter Twelve

"Who was that guy?" Zack asks as we slide into the cab of his truck. He's trying to sound casual but I know him well enough not to be fooled. I wonder if that's how I sound when I ask about Rosie.

"Just one of the ushers from the wedding. We talked for a few minutes."

I see him turn the information over in his mind. Zack's the practical type who's not going to worry about a guy on his way back to the mainland. "So how did it go this evening?"

"It was... interesting." I'm still overcome by the shock of being discovered, the fear of Mom finding out, and also the kindness and interest that the Broadmans showed me. I tell him about saving Edward Broadman and the wedding, while he maneuvers his old truck down the series of switchbacks from the Inn, asking questions as we go.

"Man! I can't believe I missed a major kelp rescue!"

Leave it to Zack to view what happened as an adventure. "Promise you won't tell anyone? Mom can't find out about this."

"I won't tell. But... way to go, Alex! That was badass!"

He'll keep his promise. Margaret also promised to keep my secret, and after tomorrow they'll be gone forever. I can relax a little, about that at least.

"The other thing is: Jenna and Dizzy can only lend me $500. So I have to find the rest somewhere else."

"Take up a collection."

"Believe me, I've thought of it." I close my eyes and lean my head back against the worn seat. We sit in a comfortable silence, while a part of my brain ponders all that old stuff in our garage. Maybe I can hold a yard sale.

Zack drives with his left hand on the wheel and his right resting on the seat between us, only a few inches away from my leg. On top of everything else that happened tonight, Zack kissed me.

Does he want to kiss me again? Jenna said Zack was trying to end it with Rosie. With him only inches away, she's fading into the background for me.

The moon teases me, shining its light into the truck's cab, as if it wants to make sure I get a good look at Zack's strong profile and the muscles moving in his arms as he turns the steering wheel. I stop thinking about yard sales.

I flick my eyes to the right side view mirror, hoping to check out my face, but see only the road rushing by. I run my tongue over my teeth and wish I had a mint or something.

At my house, Zack kills the truck's engine and gives me a sideways look. "I'll walk you to the back door."

He never does this. My throat is dry, and I'm crumbling into pieces. As we head away from the truck, he takes my hand. Our fingers interlace so deeply that I go weak in the knees.

On rubbery legs, I follow him along the narrow side path of my house and onto our back patio. All the light bulbs back there are burned out. For once, our habit of letting the place go is working for me.

I feel, rather than see, him turn to face me. I look up at him. If not for the dark, I'm sure he would see my heart pounding under the silk of Rebecca's dress. His arm slides around my waist. He smells of his spicy aftershave.

"Did you just *shave?*" I go up on my toes to sniff his neck playfully. "To pick me up at the Inn?"

"They said it was a fancy wedding. I didn't do it for you." His smile says *Of course, I did.* He pulls me toward him. "Do you like it?"

"I thought you didn't do it for me!"

"Just asking." He tightens his arms around my waist until my feet almost leave the ground. My body presses against his, and for a split second, our lips are so close I can feel his breath. Then a light attacks our eyes and he backs away from me, looking at something over my shoulder. The door opens behind me.

"Hey, Sue," he groans.

My mother stands at the top of our back steps, her bathrobe tied around her. She's in one of her bright, social moods. "Hey," she says. "What're you guys up to?"

• • •

Rebecca's green silk dress has a stain on it. It's the first thing I see upon waking up the next morning. Now I'll have to dry clean the dress, and that will cost something like sixteen bucks, which I don't have.

I'll have the money when the Broadmans pay me. Marlayne at the bank will cash the check for me, since I don't have a checking account of my own, and I'll hide some of the bills in a folder under my mattress.

I groan to myself, thinking of Zack's arms around me last night, his sexy aftershave, and how close we were to an amazing kiss until Mom showed up.

Speaking of which, it's seven o'clock on Sunday morning, and I have to get her out of bed. Mom moans and mumbles, burying her face in the pillow as I prod her shoulder.

"Two cakes today," I say in her ear in my special "wake up" voice, which I make extra piercing to punish her for ruining my moment with Zack.

I have to talk to Nate today about a loan. When I get all the money in hand, I'll just inform Mom I'm going to take the class, whether she likes it or not. It's all going to work out—I keep telling myself that.

"Get up!" I repeat, walking into the kitchen. I'm thankful she didn't see anything when she interrupted Zack and me. The other good thing is, the Broadmans will leave the island today and take my secret with them. Everything's going to be fine.

Since we'll be done delivering today's cakes by noon, I should be able to get in a late afternoon dive with Zack. We planned to dive today around Squatter's Cove. I think of last night's almost-kiss and imagine myself with Zack, swimming in the ocean, making out as the waves carry us up onto the sand.

My mother stands in the kitchen door. She's in a thin night-shirt, barefoot, shivering, her face drawn and her arms wrapped tight around herself.

"Are you okay?" I can tell she's had another one of her dreams.

She shudders. "This one was worse than usual. You were trapped down underneath the water, and I could see you, but I couldn't reach you." Her face is gray. "You were fighting to get free, but you couldn't. And I watched you…." Her voice cracks, and she doesn't finish.

"Mom." I move over to put my arms around her. "It's just a dream. That's never gonna happen to me."

"How do you know? How can you be so sure?" Mom shivers. "I hate that you dive! Why do you have to like doing dangerous things?"

"It's only dangerous if you're not careful. I'm always careful." Please don't ever let her find out about the other day.

"Have some breakfast," I say. I pour a bowl of cereal for each of us, and we sit together, eating at our little table.

"So, how was last night?" she asks after a moment. Her voice sharpens. "Did you enjoy all that fine company?"

I shrug as I bring my bowl to the sink and rinse it out. "It was a job. I worked."

"How much did the billionaires pay you?"

"I don't know. They're mailing me a check."

She stiffens. "They didn't even pay you yet?"

"Like I said, it's coming." I'm too tired to care what my mother thinks. "However much it is, I'm saving it for college."

She spoons up some cereal. "And how far do you think *that's* going to take you?"

She's right, of course. That fifty bucks, or whatever it turns out to be, won't cover most textbooks, let alone tuition. I wonder why I'm even trying.

I think again about Jenna and Dizzy and the money. She'll probably ask him today.

"Sweetie," Mom says, "I want you to go to college more than anything."

As if.

"But you already have a nice place to live, a business—a *career,* even. Why fix what isn't broken?"

"You know this isn't what I want!" I slam a drawer shut. "I'll have the van loaded in fifteen minutes."

"Alex!" she says as I head out.

"What?" I look back over my shoulder. Her face glows, her expression so hopeful that I stop my rush for the back door.

"Do you remember how I used to braid your hair? In a French braid, and put flowers in it?"

"Yeah," I say. I do remember, the feel of her fingers pinning up my hair, her scent of sugar, vanilla, cakes baking in the oven.

"I could still do it, you know. French-braid your hair, maybe for a special date?"

Where were you last night, when I needed you? "Mom. *No.* I'm almost grown up!" I see the pleading in her eyes, but ignore it. We climb into the van and take off.

As usual, I drive. My mother's on a roll now, talking nonstop. "We really need a new oven. You don't understand how old and unreliable ours is."

"Yeah, I do, Mom." I answer her automatically, hardly listening. I brake the van for a sharp turn along the winding mountain road. Straight ahead, the blue Pacific glitters, welcoming me. Directly below us—a cliff with a vertical drop of a thousand feet.

"Did you see how it shot out sparks the other day?" Her fingernails tap the window glass of the van. "And it undercooked those layers, too."

I can feel her coiling up beside me into a ball of tension. "We'll be in big trouble if we don't replace it soon."

As she talks on, my mind descends to the deepest, most quiet part of the ocean, to a place where I belong. I float there in the half-light, serene, the gentle sea creatures swimming around me. Mom's lips move, but I can't hear her. In my ears, pure silence. I'm at peace. There's not a wedding cake in sight.

• • •

At the Beachcomber, people come to help us unload our supplies. Mom's assembling an elaborate coconut four-layer cake for two hundred. Each layer will be separately covered in fondant icing to look like a wrapped gift, each with different patterns and bows.

"I'll call you when I'm almost done," she says. "Three hours at least."

Sighing inwardly, I drive off. Soon I'll be eighteen—a carefree adult with no one to think of but myself. I'm more than ready to leave behind the responsibilities of childhood.

I think of Nate and what I want to say to him about the money. He should be at his shop by now.

At Blind Man's Lookout, I stop and get out to call him. Below me, the little town of Paradise hugs the curve of its harbor—both the cove and the town are crescent-shaped. Wild, rocky hillsides, green with the last of the spring grass, rise behind the town.

Nate answers on the second ring. He and I have liked each other since the days when I worked for him to pay off my diving equipment. I picture him in his crowded shop, surrounded by racks of BCDs and boxes of fins and snorkels. He's six feet five inches and scarecrow skinny— in a wet suit, he looks like a giant Gumby doll.

"Nate, do you need someone to do your inventory for you?" Every June, Nate usually does it himself, counting every item of merchandise and making sure the physical counts match his paper records.

"I've watched you do it," I say, "and I know what's involved. It would free up your time for other things."

When I explain I'd like payment in full up front, I can almost see his eyebrows ride up his high forehead.

"This course will give me the background to design a research project for senior year." Across the water, the mainland forms a dim mountain silhouette. Beach City College is right there, somewhere under that gray blanket of haze.

He interrupts me. "Four hundred."

"Pardon?"

"Four hundred dollars up front. Start tomorrow."

"Wow, thanks!" I know he'll let me manage my own hours, so his work doesn't interfere with Mom's.

"No problem. You're a good worker." He signs off.

Two large Traveler boats pass each other outside the harbor, one leaving, one arriving. The huge catamarans glide high on their double hulls. I watch them, thinking only *eight hundred dollars left.* I'm more than halfway there.

In a few hours, Zack and I will be diving. As I gaze out at the ocean, I automatically register the weather, the wind, the look of the water. To go to Squatter's Cove, we'll need to borrow a boat from Kap Holloway, who usually lets us take his little skiff if we fill up the gas tank afterwards. I punch in Zack's number, which rings

71

five times, then goes to voice mail. At the sound of his message, I stare at the phone, as if it's transformed into an alien device in my hand.

I've never gotten Zack's voice mail. Ever. Zack always has his cell phone and always takes my calls, even if only to say he'll have to call me back. It's suddenly as if the sun didn't rise that morning.

Jenna said he wanted to break up with Rosie. I want to kiss him and talk to him about our dive at Squatter's Cove. In that order. I decide to drop by his house.

• • •

In Paradise, the houses are bungalows painted in candy colors, with no front yards. Many have front porches that border the sidewalk and second story rooftop decks, where people spend time, only eight feet up from the pavement.

I pull my van up at the tiny lavender and white house on Pomegranate Road, only to see Zack sitting on his front porch swing with Rosie. Her bare legs hang down from his lap, where she's made herself at home, relaxed and smiling, one hand toying with his hair. When they see me, all the happy smiles vanish. Zack sits up a little straighter, his eyes widening.

The breath flies out of me, as if I've been kicked in the stomach. Wanting to turn and run, I find myself rooted there in front of his house.

"Hi, Zack. Hi, Rosie." I've been on that double swing many times with Zack, although not in his lap.

"Hi, Alex," Rosie says. Her hand still plays with his hair. I wouldn't mind getting a grip on that hair myself—and giving it a good hard yank.

"Just wanted to talk about Squatter's Cove," I say to Zack. "But I can see you're busy."

He pulls himself from Rosie's clutches and comes down the steps to meet me. "It's not what you think," he says. He keeps his voice low, probably so Rosie can't hear his lame excuses.

"You know what I think? You had no business kissing me yesterday if you were planning on getting back with Rosie!"

I run and jump into the van, blinking back tears and pressing my lips together, looking down so Zack the traitor can't see my face through the windshield. I drive home, thankful that Mom's at the Beachcomber. I don't want to face her right now.

But she calls me anyway on my cell. "Alex, pick me up at two o'clock, okay? And please go to Henderson's before that. I need eight sticks of sweet butter and three cartons of eggs. And whipping cream. We're going to have to work late tonight." She hangs up.

"You're welcome," I say to the dead phone. This is one reason we're losing money, paying high island prices for ingredients at the local grocery store, just because Mom can never order the right amounts from the mainland. I wonder why we have to work late on a Sunday evening. Probably for a cheapo Monday wedding, one she booked without telling me. Weekdays are for bargain rate celebrations.

Anyway, I have school tomorrow—a last half-day of it, for us to sign each other's yearbooks before summer vacation. Tomorrow, Mom'll be on her own.

Chapter Thirteen

I dread the thought of seeing Zack and Rosie together at school the next day. Paradise High has two hundred students and is the only high school on the island. The elementary and middle schools are next door and share our lunchroom, gymnasium, and library.

The high school students hang out on a patch of asphalt called the East Yard, which the school designated especially for our use. Enclosed in chain link, with a few crooked basketball hoops, it's cruddy, but it's ours.

Rebecca's with her friend, Brooke, who played lead in the school musical. Now that I think of it, Brooke does weird hair experiments too. She's sporting a blue streak today and wears her usual nose ring.

I make my way over to them. They're both in short dresses with boots and armloads of bangles.

"Mom says to keep the dress," Rebecca says. "I never wear it."

"I don't want to take your dress." I could never admit that I'd die to have it.

"No, seriously. I don't get a good vibe off it anyway." And Rebecca and her friend wander away.

I decide to call Evelyn about it. Someday, I swear to myself, I'll be able to buy a few things of my own. I won't be a pathetic beggar forever.

Then Zack is standing by my elbow. I eye him, trying to ignore the look of his arms and shoulders in that tank top. "Where's Rosie?" I mean to say it as if I don't care, but the words come out hurt and resentful.

"*Alex.*" Zack wets his lips with his tongue and shifts from foot to foot. I've never seen him look so unhappy. "Look, about yesterday, Rosie came by the house ..."

"It's okay," I say quickly. "You and Rosie, it's for the best. Saturday, at the Inn, what happened with us was a mistake."

"A *mistake?*" Zack's looking at me with a strange expression.

"Well, I mean, you got back with Rosie two minutes later, so what else could it be?"

He seems to struggle for words. As more and more students enter the yard, we walk off into a corner where it's quiet, at the intersection of two lengths of chain link fence. Zack puts a hand up and weaves his fingers through the chain link.

"But we'll still be diving buddies, right?" I say, faking cheerfulness. I can't imagine life without Zack, his friendship, the love we both have for the island, our ocean adventures. I look up at him, taking in his wild man hair and green eyes, which are suddenly intense in their expression.

"Is that what you really want?" he asks. "To be diving buddies?"

"Yeah, sure." I shrug. "Like always, right?" Why stick my neck out when I know he likes Rosie better?

His face closes up. "Okay, then." For a moment we stand there, in our silent bubble, the sounds of talk and laughter around us.

"Kap Holloway wants me to work for him this summer," Zack finally says and all of a sudden we switch back to our old comfortable roles.

Our eyes meet, acknowledging what it would mean to him to work for Kap—that he's starting down the road toward his dream.

All Zack has ever wanted is to run his own charter dive operation here on Santa Rita.

"He wants you, too—when you're eighteen," Zack continues, with a bleak look. That won't happen until September, three months from now.

Rosie materializes beside Zack, wearing sleek leggings and a little shirt that seems to hug her body in all the right places. I look down at my sweat pants and faded Nate's Dive Shop T-shirt. No wonder he chose her.

"Zack," she says, "We have to go in now." She pulls him off to class, leaving me alone to picture him riding off into the sunset with her and Kap Holloway, while I spend the rest of my life with my mother, the two of us dowel-sticked and frosted together like the layers of a wedding cake.

• • •

Roy looks up from his cluttered desk. My science teacher throughout high school, it was he who talked the Dean at Beach City College into letting me attend their summer oceanography class as a special exception. "They want you to enroll with them after you finish high school," he told me. "Beach City doesn't usually get students of your caliber."

On the wall behind Roy are photos of his wife and two young boys. A mobile of the planets in our solar system turns slowly in a corner near the ceiling.

"Hey, Alex," he says.

Still stinging from all the bad news of the last few days, I slide into a chair by the door. "I just dropped by to say 'have a good summer'."

Roy squints at me and feels around for his glasses on the top of the gray, metal desk. "I'm glad you did." His hand closes on them and brings them up to his face. "There you are!"

He turns the full power of his smile— wide and sincere—on me. "I hear congratulations are in order!"

I sit up, alarmed. What has he heard?

"Beach City College," he says. "I got a call from Dean Lowell over there. He's really glad you'll be attending this summer. So's Henry."

"You told Mr. Perez?" I almost wail. Henry Perez is our high school principal.

"Yeah. Dean Lowell has a call in to the president of the college. "They're really excited to have you!"

I find myself staring at a stain on the wall over his head. Eight hundred more dollars. Mom would never notice if I sold my old bike from grade school. Maybe Henderson's groceries would advance me wages if I promised to work this summer.

"That's great," I hear myself say.

Roy and I leave the school together and wish each other a good summer. I walk away telling myself over and over again that it'll be fine.

Chapter Fourteen

The next day I go out on a mission to find merchants in town willing to loan me money in exchange for work. Mom's still sleeping when I leave the house. It's a wedding-free Tuesday, so we're just going to bake layers in the afternoon.

"I'd hire you in a minute," Dixie, the manager at Henderson's Groceries, tells me, "but if I gave you an advance on salary, all my other clerks would want one, too."

Dixie lifts weights in her spare time and could probably pick me up and bench press me without breaking a sweat. Her biceps strain against the short sleeves of her Henderson's Groceries shirt.

"Listen, there's a rumor going around," she says, "that you're the person who saved that rich guy." She looks me over, as if I'm wearing the answer to her question.

"Wow. Crazy rumor, huh?" I flee. I should go home and talk to Mom, but I have to find eight hundred dollars. Today. And she's probably still sleeping.

I visit four more stores, but all anyone wants to talk about is me, the hero. Don at the Super Scoop says, "I always knew you were going places!" He asks someone to take a photo of him and me next to the giant free-standing plywood ice cream cone in front of his shop.

I go by the bank to ask about loans. "We're so proud of you, Alex!" Trish and Marlayne tell me. "Were you really scared? Were you in danger?"

On Carousel Avenue, people stop me three times to talk, and each time a crowd gathers to congratulate me. By now, it's one o'clock, and my worry about Mom and my equipment overtakes my worry about the eight hundred dollars. I rush home.

Mom greets me with hands on her hips, pale with fury.

"Alexandra! I've had nothing but phone calls this morning. You better tell me what's going on, and fast!"

"What do you mean?" I give her a bland look.

"You went diving alone? After you told me you never would?"

I close my eyes. For someone who's supposed to be smart, I've been seriously stupid. Panic pumps its way through my veins. "I saved a man's life, Mom!"

"Yes. So I hear. What were you doing down there alone? When I think what could have happened to you...." Her eyes reflect back to me all the terrible possibilities that are in her mind.

"It was just that one time. I'll never do it again! I promise!"

Mom is shaking her head slowly. "You made me a promise before, and you broke it. Things could have gone very differently that day." Again, her eyes have that look of fear in them, the fear of what could have been.

A terrible sick feeling is growing in my stomach. "You're not going to...?"

"I *have*, Alexandra. I warned you about this. I will do *anything* to keep you safe!"

No. I turn on my heel and run out to the little free-standing garage behind our house, where I keep my dive equipment. I tear through the door, skidding to a stop by the bin that usually holds my fins, octopus rig, BCD, weight belt, and wet suit. They're gone. Without asking for my side of things or giving me a second chance, she has taken my most precious belongings away.

It's like losing a friend. I keep looking for my things, rooting around through the boxes, old sports equipment, rags, gardening tools, hoping to find them still there, maybe hidden away somewhere as a lesson to me.

Mom walks up behind me and touches my shoulder, but I wrench myself away. "Do you know how dangerous it is to dive alone?" she says. "I'd be destroyed if I lost you!"

"Where's my stuff?"

"You don't need to know that!"

"That was *mine*!" I scream. "You had *no right!*"

"Don't talk to me about your rights." She pushes her face into mine. "And what's this about you attending Beach City College? What kind of stories are you spreading?"

A wave of nausea runs over me. "Where did you hear that?"

"The Paradise Gazette called. They're running an article tomorrow." Mom's voice is thin and strained. "About the wonderful Alex Marshall and all her accomplishments."

"Oh my God!" I jump to my feet. "They can't write that! About Beach City!"

"Too late. You've got some *big* explaining to do."

"You have to let me go then! That'll fix this whole thing!"

"Nope. You created this problem. You handle it." Mom looks sorry, but not that sorry.

So, there in my kitchen, with Mom standing over me, I have to call Roy and tell him it isn't true. I'm not going to attend Beach City College this summer.

"I'm really sorry, Roy. I appreciate your helping me get admitted. I wish I could have done it."

There's a short silence on his end. "What happened, Alex?"

"I have to help my mom instead. And then, there's the money…" My throat aches and my eyes water, and my whole body quivers from the disappointment.

"Your mother won't help you?"

I don't answer.

"I'm sorry," he says. "I know how much it meant to you."

Again, I don't answer, unable to speak. Is there a way to save my research project? My mind already races for ideas.

"I'll call Henry. And then the Dean," he says. "But you'll have to call them first." He adds, speaking carefully, "The College was really excited you were coming."

"Okay." My voice sounds small and miserable, but not half as much as I feel. "Are they going to be mad at you, Roy?"

He hesitates ever so little. "Don't worry about it."

Feeling like a something dirty on the bottom of a shoe, I call the Dean of Life Sciences at Beach City. He listens in total silence as I stammer and stutter my way through my explanation, ending with, "I'm really sorry."

"I'm sorry, too," he says. His voice is cool and impersonal. "Good luck with your future plans."

I hang up, staring blindly ahead of me. Disappointment and anger roll around inside me, coiling my insides into knots.

"Alex...," my mother says, reaching out a hand.

I recoil. "Don't touch me! Don't ever speak to me again!"

I push past her and run out of the house and up Cinnamon Street, away from the water, then turn on Pomegranate Road toward Zack's house. He, of all people, will understand. People on their front decks and verandas call out to me as I run past, but I wave and keep running. At Zack's place, I bound up the front steps and across the porch, pound on the door, then—as I've done hundreds of times before—turn the knob and walk in.

"Hello?" I call, my breathing ragged.

After a few seconds, Zack comes out of his bedroom, adjusting the waistband of his gym shorts. Since the curtains are drawn, it's dark in the living room where I'm standing. I see him framed for an instant in the lit opening of the hallway, then he moves toward me.

"What's wrong?" he asks.

I start to cry. "Mom took away my dive equipment. And I can't go to Beach City. And I let Roy down!" I stand there with my arms wrapped around myself, sniffling, and staring up at Zack, while his eyes darken. He puts his arms around me and I find myself with my face against his skin, leaking tears down his chest. He's almost naked, in nothing but a pair of old gym shorts.

"God, Alex," he says. But something's wrong. Something makes me pull away from him.

"Maybe I shouldn't have come," I say, "but I was so upset."

"It's okay," he says, as Rosie's head appears in the doorway of his bedroom. Her hair's down, and tangled. As she steps out into the hallway, I see she's wearing one of Zack's tank tops, apparently also hastily pulled on, with nothing underneath.

"Zack, what's going on?" she says.

He wavers, his eyes shifting back and forth between the two of us. Finally, he says, "Rosie, I'm sorry. I need a minute with Alex. Please?" She disappears.

I want to sink down through the floor. "I shouldn't have come," I repeat. My insides churning, I'm stumble over my own feet in my haste to get out of there.

Zack follows me. "Don't go."

"What do you mean, 'don't go?' There's a naked girl in your bedroom!"

He sees my point. "I'll call you. We'll figure out something about your equipment."

"No. I'm sorry. It's not your problem." I try to keep my voice level as I say it, although I feel like screaming the words at him.

I run down the steps of his house and down the hill toward the harbor, turning when I reach the Seawalk and running along the edge of the water.

I can't go to college, can't be with Zack. Can't dive anymore.

Now that it's summer, most of the slips in Paradise Harbor hold private sailboats and yachts, whose owners live aboard. Wagging his tail, a dog barks at me from a boat called the Lady Louise.

I've done everything all wrong.

As I run, my feet and heart pound in separate but steady rhythms.

Blew it. Blew it. Blew it. My feet pound out the message.

The people at Beach City College think I'm a total flake. They're not going to be making exceptions for me again anytime soon.

And what did I ever do to deserve my mother? Her face is in front of me, her eyes, the way they looked just now.

Pure terror.

I'd be destroyed if I lost you.

I run on, past the harbor and along the ocean's edge out to the heliport. Here, I have the road to myself, along with a few seagulls who've landed on stones down by the water.

Blew it. Blew it. I keep running, thinking if I don't stop I'll eventually run myself to death and put myself out of my misery. *Blew it.* But after another half mile or so, the harsh message grows softer.

I've never been a quitter. I'll get over Zack, I tell myself. A mental finger pokes me, and a little voice says, *You can do it.*

My muscles warm up and my breathing steadies.

I'll keep the inventory job this summer and build my college fund. So what if I can't take the Beach City class? I'll design a research project anyway, and somehow, I'll start diving again. *I can do it.* Most important of all, I'll figure out a way to get through to Mom.

After a few moments, the beating of my heart and the striking of my feet upon the pavement turn the words into a new refrain that I repeat to myself as I run along. *I can do it. I can do it.*

A breeze passes, carrying a mist from the ocean that feels cool on my face. The mid-day glare has mellowed into the slanting rays of the late afternoon. Someone on a nearby yacht uncorks a champagne bottle, making a loud pop, followed by exclamations and laughter.

As I change direction and head back the way I came—toward my mother, our unkempt home, and the endless stream of wedding cakes—I repeat the words to myself over and over again.

I can do it. I can do it. I can do it.

Chapter Fifteen

My picture, with a big article, appears in The Paradise Gazette. It mentions Beach City once and otherwise focuses on how I saved Edward Broadman. Everywhere I go, people stop me for the story and congratulate me. They say how proud my mother must be.

Wrong. The more praise and attention I receive, the more insistent she gets. "What you did was foolish and dangerous. You could have died! Thank goodness you're not diving anymore."

I don't respond. Forget oceanography. I need a class in Mother Management. I have to get through to my mother, and I don't know where to start.

Over Mom's protests, I begin my inventory job for Nate. "It won't interfere with my work for you," I promise her. Nate gives me a key to the shop, and whenever I have a spare hour or two, I run over and count diving masks. When he pays me, the first thing I do is take out sixteen dollars to dry clean Rebecca's dress. Or rather, my dress, which Evelyn has told me to keep.

In other spare moments, I list ideas for research projects and set myself a deadline of two weeks to come up with three good ideas to present to Roy.

But the way Mom does things, it's hard to manage my time. Because she often forgets to order supplies and put her updates on my computer spreadsheets, our lives are a constant stream of last minute disasters. To make matters worse, our oven keeps sparking and heating up however it wants to, which means some days the layers didn't turn out right and have to be redone.

A week goes by in an endless stream of eggs, sugar, flour, cake batter, piping bags, and anxious brides. I do my work, take long runs every day, and speak to Mom as little as I have to. I'm stuck, not knowing what to do about her. The few times that Zack calls me, I don't call him back.

Every day, I scope our P.O. Box for the Broadmans' check, not that it will make a material difference in my life, but to remind me that it truly happened, that once upon a time I really was a hero.

• • •

Our post office box holds a slip saying we have a package. Thinking it's probably one of my mother's numerous mail order purchases of kitchen trinkets, jewelry, or lingerie, I stand in line at the window.

Our postmistress, Annabelle Meadows, is like a large Jello-mold. She's sweet and every part of her quivers—her voice, her corkscrew curls, her multiple chins.

"Alex, you've gotten two big packages! And a smaller third one! And they're from the Broadmans!" Behind me in line, Brady, who was at Dizzy's with Darryl that night, and Pete Ferguson, who's married to Brady's sister, crane their necks over me toward the counter.

They are good-sized boxes, not the check-containing envelope I was expecting. "They don't rattle when you shake them, they just shift around some," Annabelle reports.

"Thanks, Annabelle," I say, disappointing her by not ripping the boxes open on the spot.

"They probably wanted to thank you for saving the old man's life," Brady says, peering nearsightedly at the boxes through his wire-rimmed glasses.

"Maybe it's a couple o' hams," Pete offers. His beer belly, spilling over his belt, presses against the post office counter.

"But then what's in that third box?" Brady asks.

"All right, see you guys." I smile and wave, pulling at one of the boxes. They're heavy, even for me. I could carry them one at a time, but the two guys insist on helping me with them out to the van.

"Thanks!" I hop in the van and zoom away, ignoring their dejected faces. Since I can't take the boxes to my house or Zack's, I drive up Sasparilla Street to Jenna and Dizzy's little Victorian-style cottage with its white picket fence and blue shutters. They're sitting at their kitchen table having lunch when I knock on their back door with a box in my arms.

"Come in, honey," Jenna calls through the screen door, getting up from the table to help me. As she passes her husband, she gives his shoulder a squeeze just as he shoots an arm out and catches her by the waist. Dizzy Malone, ruddy-complexioned with a walrus mustache, is the younger brother of Zack's dad, Spike.

"This is from the Broadmans," I say. "There are two more in the van." I put the box on the kitchen floor, while Dizzy brings in the others.

"Good heavens, Alex, it looks like Christmas in June," Jenna says as boxes fill the small kitchen.

Sun snakes its way through the Venetian blinds, laying stripes across the hanging macramé baskets of plants, gingham tablecloth, and old-fashioned wallpaper with pictures of peppermills, teapots, and cookie jars. While Jenna and Dizzy watch, I slide a scissor along the box edges, cutting the tape, then lift the flaps. In one box, two envelopes lie on top, which I pick up and put aside as my eyes go automatically to the contents of the boxes.

It's like discovering a treasure chest. In one box, carefully wrapped, are expensive dive computers—five of them. There are five octopus rigs and BCDs, all slick recent models, and in the second box are the wet suits, fins, and masks to go with them. The smaller, heavy third box holds the weight belts. It's thousands of dollars of primo diving equipment, barely used and in perfect condition.

"Darn it, we have to go back to work," Jenna says. As they start for the door, I call out to them.

"Don't tell anyone what's in these boxes! Please!"

They stop, Dizzy with one hand on the doorknob, and Jenna with one arm in the sleeve of her jacket. "Why not?" Dizzy asks.

I have to tell them. "Mom took away all my diving equipment, and she would take this, too, if she found out about it."

"Really," Jenna says, in a strangled voice. She's late for her shift at the Inn, and Dizzy has to open the Dive for Lunchtime Karaoke.

"We won't tell anyone for now," Dizzy says, "but we need to understand what's going on. Be here for dinner tonight?"

"Okay." I breathe a little easier. They'll give me good advice.

They leave me alone with my riches. I can't believe my good luck. I can dive again. I can keep whatever works for me out of this equipment and take the rest over to Nate at the Dive Shop, who'll make me a sweet deal for it. I'll keep one of the dive computers, for sure, and give one to Zack, I think, but then I remember that he's not a part of my life anymore.

I look at the two envelopes. The top one says simply "Alexandra" in a spidery handwriting. The envelope's a creamy white, with the inititals MDB in dark gray. Inside is a folded sheet of the same creamy white paper.

Dear Alexandra:

The Broadman women have decided that perhaps diving is something our men should stay away from. We collected all the equipment in the family, and now bequeath it to you. We thought you might have a use for these items. Do with them what you wish.

More important, dear girl, please know that you are a very special young lady. We are—I am— forever in your debt. In the other enve-

lope is a token of thanks that we hope will also be of use to you. Believe me, it is small compared to what you have done for us.

We will stay in touch, I promise.

With warmest regards,
Margaret Broadman

My eyes prickle as I read the letter. I had almost started to believe it never happened, that it was only a dream. They've apparently sent the payment for my work at the wedding. We never actually agreed on a price, but I put in seven hours of work. I'm betting they'll pay well, maybe even eight or ten dollars an hour. The second envelope's in Broadman Enterprises stationery, with "Miss Alexandra Marshall" typed across the back. I open it, pull out the check inside, and scream.

It's for ten thousand dollars.

• • •

I lie on my bed, looking at my check. I want to kiss it. It seems like a fortune, enough money to last a lifetime.

Of course, I know what I'll do with it. Now I'll have a serious college fund. I can hardly believe it.

Then I realize something.

I have no checking account. I have no savings account. I have to be eighteen to get an account without my mother's signature. If I walk into the Paradise bank with a check for ten thousand dollars, Marlayne and Trish will hand it right back to me, and tell the entire town about it while they're at it.

It's a given that, if my mom learns about the check, she'll have ideas how to spend it. We always need things, are always behind on one payment or another. I've never been able to save any extra money I earned, because we were always short on the rent or needed new tires for the van or had to buy my schoolbooks.

In the past, I've sneaked a few small checks to Trish or Marlayne, who've quietly cashed them for me. As I feel hysteria begin to mount, I consider doing this with a check for ten thousand dollars. I'm not sure if our little branch bank even has that much cash in it.

And even if I can get ten thousand dollars in cash, where on earth would I keep it? I only have so much room under my mattress. It makes no sense. I have to have a bank account.

I lie on my bed for a long time, going over my options. Finally, I admit to myself that I'm screwed. I have a check for ten thousand dollars and nowhere to put it. I slide the check into an envelope and place it under my mattress, a dream that won't be coming true, at least for now.

In three months, I tell myself, I'll be eighteen and can do whatever I want. I can take off, go anywhere, never speak to my mother again. But if I do, what'll happen to her?

Zack keeps saying that I baby Mom and let her get away with stuff. "How come she needs you to get her out of bed?" he demanded once. "That's bogus!"

"It's self-preservation," I told him. If I let Mom oversleep and screw up the day's schedule, I suffer as much as she does—more, even. It's easier to just take charge. "I'll never be able to leave her. Unless I retrain her. Or find a replacement for myself."

Mom needs someone to take care of her. A fairy godmother. I wonder if such a thing can be found online—fairy godmothers for rent. Maybe I can advertise for a caretaker/ pastry chef assistant.

It would have to be exactly the right person. A very unusual person.

Who would come out to a small island and work for free.

Face it, I tell myself. It would take a miracle.

• • •

"Diving alone? That doesn't sound like you," Jenna says. "You're always so responsible." She ladles out bowls of her Champion Chili while Dizzy pours himself a beer and me a glass of water.

"I *am* responsible! I made one mistake, and I'll never do it again." I take my place at the dinner table, trying to keep the desperation out of my voice. The Broadmans' gifts have given me the chance to turn my life around. I can't lose them now.

"I don't feel right, though, about helping you to sneak around and lie to your mom, even if we do think she's being kinda nuts," Dizzy says.

Jenna shakes her head, her long hair swinging from side to side. "Of *course*, we're not going to encourage her to do things behind her mom's back. But we can help her store this stuff, don't you think? Just until Sue comes to her senses."

"Thanks, you guys." I feel lighter, as if I've just set down one of Mom's heavy boxes.

"I'm so proud of you I could bust some buttons," Jenna says. "You saved a man's life!"

Steps sound on the back porch, the door flies open, and there's Zack, standing in the kitchen doorway. Despite the open windows and the overhead ceiling fan, I feel my face flush.

"Hey, sweetie!" Jenna says to him, throwing me a sideways glance. She and Dizzy are smart enough to have figured out something's wrong between Zack and me. "We were just about to have brownies. Come sit!"

"Hey, Alex. I didn't know you were gonna be here." Zack hangs in the doorway for a minute, filling the opening with his height and broad shoulders. Then he steps through, his eyes searching mine.

"You two go sit in the living room," Jenna says. "Dizzy and I'll be along in a minute with dessert." I sink into Dizzy's old armchair, and Zack sits down on the sofa.

"What's up?" I say, relieved to hear myself sounding calm and on top of things. Something passes between us, that old bond of friendship, maybe, and all of a sudden, we're grinning at each other like idiots.

"It's really good to see you," he says.

"Yeah." It is. Good to see him, that is. Incredibly good. He looks so gorgeous and different and familiar all at the same time. But he chose Rosie over me.

"How's everything with Kap?"

"Great. Fantastic." He brightens as he tells me about his beginning as a deck hand on Kap's boat, the Sea Princess. It sounds so amazing, getting paid to be out on the water every day. I can't help it— as he talks, jealousy begins to worm its way through me. After feeling so good just a minute ago, now I start to feel ugly and unimportant. I study the pictures on Jenna and Dizzy's walls. They have some painted landscapes from a flea market and framed embroidery pieces that Jenna made years ago. "Welcome to Our Home," one of them says.

"What about Rosie? How's it going?" I ask the question because I genuinely think I'm fine, that I have it together and can talk about this without losing it. But my voice gets thin and then cracks, and I have to fake a coughing fit.

Zack gives me a faint grin. "We're good. We don't fight as much as we used to."

"Congratulations… I think?" A little bubble of happiness rises in me. He doesn't exactly sound swept away by passion. Another of the embroidery pieces carries the words, "Count your Blessings Every Day."

"How about you?" he asks. "How's it going with Sue?"

I shrug. "Just trying to make cakes. Our oven's sparked a couple of times and can't always hold a temperature. So it's getting harder and harder."

Zack looks at me in alarm. "That's dangerous. You need to replace it."

"We don't have enough saved yet." Of course, that's not exactly true. I have the Broadman money. But after what Mom did to me, I'm keeping my mouth shut and hiding my loot under my mattress.

"Anyone wanna play gin rummy?" Dizzy calls from the kitchen. He's shuffling a pack of cards.

Zack stands up. "Nah, I gotta be going."

I stay for a while, talking to Jenna and Dizzy and playing cards. "Thanks so much, you guys," I say to them as I leave. But as I walk home, something else occurs to me. It doesn't matter whether Jenna and Dizzy help me keep the equipment. I've lost my dive partner. I can't dive without a partner.

I walk home, go straight into my bedroom, and shut the door.

• • •

I pluck up my courage and call Roy for the first time since the fiasco. "I was thinking," I say, "I still want to do that research project next year. I was hoping I could go over some of my ideas with you."

I can almost feel his interest crackle along the phone line. "Sure! But it'll have to be in a couple of weeks. We're leaving with the kids on vacation today."

We agree on a date, and I hang up. I can't start work on this until I talk to Roy. Feeling restless, I start cleaning our house. I figure even if I can never afford to buy a home of my own, I still don't have to live like a barn animal. I throw away all the take-out garbage, dust the shelves and tables, do the laundry. I vacuum and mop floors. Our home isn't fancy or well furnished, but now it's clean and tidy.

The next day, I find a pile of May bills on Mom's desk, all unpaid. Trivial items, like our rent, power, and water, not to mention the bill from our wholesale baking supplier. I total up the amounts due to find that, as per usual, they exceed our bank balance.

I flag down Mom. "Look what I found."

Her eyebrows knit together. "Where were they?"

"On your desk."

"I was so sure I'd paid them." Flustered, she riffles through them. "We owe so much! I don't even know where to start."

We sit down together and pay in full the most important checks—rent and utilities. We make partial payments to suppliers and credit cards and finish with fifty-five dollars in our checking account.

"We should have some payments coming in soon," I tell Mom, trying not to feel guilty about the ten thousand dollars I'm hoarding under my mattress. "We'll be fine."

"What would I ever do without you?" She gives me a sad smile.

"Mom, we've got to make a system for you to follow. Like, all the bills go in one place. Then, twice a month, you sit down and pay them." We find a shoe box and label it "Unpaid Bills."

I put it on the corner of her desk. "All bills go there now. And on the first, we'll sit down and go through them, okay?"

Mom nods, obediently.

"By the way, I made us an appointment next Saturday at 10:00," I say. "This guy's coming with his daughter to order a cake." It's Lester Lindstrom, the man I met the morning of the Broadman wedding.

"Okay, but I can't stay the whole time." She signs the last check and hands it to me. "Manicure appointment at 10:30."

I sigh. And there, with that manicure, goes the last money in our checking account.

I fantasize about the money from the Broadmans, imagine myself somehow setting up an account, Zack coming to his senses and leaving Rosie. I see the two of us diving together in places like Australia and the Red Sea, climbing mountains in Nepal. I feel his kiss again and his hands in my hair.

I start doing my nails and putting moisturizer on my face. I brush my hair and let it fall to the middle of my back. I might end up an uneducated block-head, but I'll look good doing it. Maybe the next time Zack sees me he'll eat his heart out, the traitor.

When a text message comes through on my cell phone, I'm lying on my bed, reading. I sit up and click on the text message. "I'm coming to the island this weekend. Can I see U?"

My eyes widen in surprise.

It's from Jeremy Broadman.

Chapter Sixteen

Jeremy barrels off the Santa Rita Traveler, lugging a guitar case and duffel bags, with a wide grin on his face. I'm trying to remember how I ended up agreeing to pick up this guy I barely know from the boat terminal. We were texting back and forth, and somehow it just happened.

I can't say I mind, though. A tingle of anticipation runs through me.

He seems different. It's not his clothes, because he wears loafers, khakis, and a polo shirt, like the first time I saw him. He's different in another way, more awake somehow. Or more engaged.

"Alex!" He gives me a kiss, first on one cheek, then the other, French-style. He's looking around him in a happy, excited way, as if he's thrilled to be here. Not what I'd expect from a jaded billionaire boy who's been everywhere.

Meanwhile, the eyes of a half dozen locals are on me as I air kiss this cute stranger right under their noses. Even I'm wondering what I'm doing here. Why did he call me anyway? Is he interested in me?

In my mind I hear my mother's voice. *He doesn't know anyone else out here.*

We walk away from the terminal toward my van. "How long are you staying?"

"Two months."

"*Two months?*" That news'll get tongues flapping about either his romantic or his spending potential, depending upon your age group.

"Where are you going to stay all that time?" Housing on the island's always in short supply.

"The Inn."

Even for the Broadmans, it's an expensive way to go. "How'd you manage that?" We throw his stuff in the back of my van and head up Mt. Vazquez toward his new home.

"They have an extra guest room up on the top level, where the manager lives. They keep it unrented usually, for emergencies. So anyway, they agreed to let me have it for eight weeks."

I don't get it. As much as I love Santa Rita, I don't know why this guy wants to spend eight weeks here when he could go anywhere in the world.

"Alex, you have to help get me a job," Jeremy's saying.

He's mega rich. He doesn't need a job. I don't say it, but Jeremy must have picked up on my thought.

"In my family, you work," he says. "That's the way we are."

I pull into a guest parking slot in front, as Evelyn and Rebecca walk out to greet us. The Inn has a set of wide front steps lined with planter boxes leading up to a white door inset with leaded glass. Beyond the door, I catch a glimpse of the Inn's rich draperies and hardwood floors.

"Jeremy, we would have picked you up," Evelyn says, while Rebecca hovers behind her in over-sized cargo pants and a t-shirt that she seems to have attacked with a pair of scissors.

"No worries. I got Alex to do it." He sees Rebecca. "Hi."

She manages a nod.

He swivels back in my direction. "So, you wanna see my new digs?"

"Sure!" Does Jeremy like me? All my life, I've hung with boys, but it's been on bikes and skateboards or forty feet under water. I've never had a guy like me as a girl. The closest I came was Zack, and he ran to Rosie the second he got a chance.

Evelyn leads the way. Jeremy acts the gentleman and gestures me to walk ahead of him, which gives me another little tingle. Rebecca silently falls in behind Jeremy as we go upstairs.

The tour of Jeremy's room, completely filled by an antique dresser and cast-iron bed, takes under thirty seconds. As Jeremy sets his guitar case in a corner, Rebecca speaks her first words: "What kind of guitar do you have?"

He lays the case out on the bed and opens it for her.

"Wow!" Rebecca stares at it.

It looks like an ordinary guitar to me, but you'd think Rebecca had just discovered a secret cache of gold.

"Do you play?" Jeremy asks her.

"Yeah, but not a guitar like that!"

Funny, I'd never realized Rebecca was into music. I check in with my mother, then head off with Jeremy to Dizzy's for lunch and to find out if Dizzy needs bus boys. Again, I wonder why he wants to bus dishes at Dizzy's Dive when he could be touring the pyramids or cruising the Greek islands.

Jeremy drives me down the switchbacks from the Inn, using the golf cart he's rented for the next eight weeks. He looks all around him, excited as a kid with his new toy. His good mood is rubbing off on me, and I feel better than I have all summer.

Maybe we'll get to know each other. Become friends. Maybe more than friends. But then, I hear my mother's voice again. *We don't belong with people like them.*

We reach Dizzy's door, with its sign reading "Sorry, We're Open," and enter, both of us stopping for a minute to let our eyes adjust to the light. "We'll eat at the bar," I tell him.

Jeremy checks out the décor. "Interesting use of dead sea life," he notes in a low voice, as we pass a swordfish and a lobster posing together on a fishnet.

"You making fun of our island ways?" I'm only half-joking.

"Nope," he says. "This place rocks." We weave our way through the tables and find two stools at the bar.

"But, seriously, Jeremy, what's the big deal with Santa Rita Island? I'll bet you've traveled all over the world."

"Oh, you know. New places. New people."

I can't tell if I'm imagining it, or if he's avoiding my question. He drums on the bar with his hands. "Now all I need's a job."

"But, why bus tables, when you could do anything?"

"Like I said, it's something new." He has become a blank, impenetrable wall.

Dizzy walks up to us. "There's my girl," he says to me. He wears a large button saying, "I have a degree in liberal arts. Do you want fries with that?"

"Nice to meet you," Jeremy says. "You're Alex's uncle?" He shows no signs of an arrogant rich boy slumming it for the summer. I can see Dizzy giving him a point for that.

"No, I'm Zack's uncle." Dizzy doesn't seem to notice Jeremy's look of confusion. "But Alex is like family to me."

"Well, sir, I was wondering if you have work for me."

"You ever waited tables?"

"No. But I think I could figure it out pretty fast."

Dizzy looks him over. "This is the deal. If you're willing to be on call for a few weeks, and if you work out, maybe I can give you a shift." He shoots a stern look at Jeremy. "No guarantees, though, and you have to be real available for the on-call work."

"I'll do it. Thanks." To my astonishment, Jeremy looks pleased. "By the way, that's an excellent button. I'll remember it as I head off to college."

"It's part of my collection."

"Dizzy has the largest collection of buttons in the western world," I tell Jeremy. "He and the waiters wear different ones every day."

"Outstanding," Jeremy says. "You should get bumper stickers for your walls."

97

Dizzy gives a startled laugh. "That's not a half bad idea."

It's twelve o'clock, and Lunchtime Karaoke's beginning. A horde of pale-faced city folk, already half sloshed, roils around the sign-up list.

"Karaoke! This place gets better and better." Jeremy's eyes sparkle. "Say you'll do it with me."

"*No!* What's wrong with you?" I swivel my stool around to give him a mock glare. Karaoke's for mainlanders.

He heaves a sigh. "I thought you were *fun*, Alex."

"Believe me, there's nothing fun about hearing me sing."

I have to get home and do the baking for the weekend. As we head back up the hill to the Inn, where I've left my van, Jeremy asks, "Who's Zack?"

"What do you mean?"

"Well, Dizzy mentioned him as if I would know who he was."

"He's a friend," I say, sounding shorter than I'd meant to.

"Was that the guy who showed up the night of the wedding? To pick you up?"

I nod.

"Is he your boyfriend?"

"No. He has a girlfriend." I'm horrified by how sad I sound.

Jeremy glances over at me and lets it drop. He leaves me at my van, saying, "Listen, can I call you? It's nice to know someone out here."

I realize I want him to call me. "Sure. How about snorkeling at the Point sometime?"

His face lights up. "Love to. I'll talk to you tomorrow."

I can't figure him out exactly, but he's fun, and I sure could use some of that.

Chapter Seventeen

"This is a nice one," Lester Lindstrom says. He points to a shot in our portfolio of a brightly colored cake with a seashell theme. He and his daughter Jessica sit in our newly clean living room trying to decide on a wedding cake.

I'm wondering why he's making serious eye contact with my mom when their client information card refers to a Mr. and Mrs. Lester Lindstrom. Maybe he's not as nice as I thought he was.

"I'd like to have orchids on my cake," Jessica says. She's a skinny little thing and wears a yellow blouse and plaid skirt. She looks barely older than I am—way too young to be planning a wedding. I glance down at their card again. She's twenty-one.

"We can do an orchid cake for you. Do you want them fresh or made of frosting?" Mom's dressed for clients, in a simple peach-colored shift, her hair pulled up except for some escaped curls that frame her face. Her makeup makes her hazel eyes look green.

"I never thought of frosting orchids."

"I could make some samples and send you photographs."

"Wow, Jess, look at this!" Lester studies a photo of a six-layer cake with frosting lilies cascading down the side. He wears a short-sleeved shirt and is super freckled. If it weren't for small amounts of white skin peeking out between the freckles, I would think he had a great tan.

"I need a shot of that!" Jessica photographs the page with her cell phone and fires it off in an email.

Within a few seconds, her fiance is on the phone.

"I know, baby, I wish you were here too!" Her face pinches up. "He had to work this weekend," she moans to me as she clicks off the phone.

"You're incredibly talented," Lester says to my mom, turning the pages of our display book. "I can't believe you made all these!"

Mom gives him a genuine, warm smile. I've never seen her look so relaxed and happy around a man. For that matter, I've never seen a man pay her a compliment before or show an interest in her work.

She turns to a section at the back of the book. "These are my one-of-kind cakes—all custom orders."

Lester exclaims as he bends over the pages, turning them slowly to see cakes with hand-painted designs, textured frostings, sprays of sugar calla lilies, daisies, magnolias.

He flashes Mom his wide gap-toothed grin. "Did you go to cooking school?"

"I'm self-taught," Mom answers carefully. She's always been insecure about her lack of education.

"You really *are* talented then. To learn all that on your own. I personally have no artistic inclinations."

I haven't noticed it before, but he's actually cute—for an old guy who's kind of nerdy. I don't know if it's the smile, or just the way he looks at her, all warm and interested, leaning forward, as if he wants to hear everything she has to say.

He's into her. The thought grabs me and won't let go.

"What do you do then?" Mom asks him.

"Both myself and my wife are accountants."

"'Oh! I see!" Mom says, sitting back in her chair.

At least he's honest.

"Should I bring in some tasting samples?" I ask.

Mom jumps to her feet. "Yes," she blurts, not looking in Lester's direction, "Alex is going to handle this part of it. I'm afraid I have an appointment in town." She rushes off to her manicure.

I serve them a silver platter of Tiny Cakes, prepared the way Mom taught me, with small cubes of cake, a thin layer of frosting and a rosette on each, and around the edges of the tray, leaves and strawberries. Lester and Jessica both exclaim when they see it.

"It looks like you lifted it right out of a magazine," Lester says. Jessica emails off another photo, while he puts a coconut sample in his mouth. "I do like sweets," he confesses.

"Mmm." Jessica closes her eyes as she bites into a sample. "Mom would love this one."

"Did your mother have to work this weekend, too?" I ask her.

Lester clears his throat and blinks a few times. "Lorraine and I have actually been separated for two years. Her company transferred her to North Carolina recently, so Jess is stuck with my help for the wedding."

He's separated. Like a squirrel on a nut, my brain snatches up the information and stores it in a safe place, to be inspected later.

Jessica jumps in. "He's a great wedding consultant! He's even in charge of the centerpieces and bouquet!"

"That's just because I know orchids." Lester gives Jessica a fond look.

My eyes burn as I see the easy respect and affection between them. "Orchids?"

"It's our hobby," Jessica says. "My dad and I grow them in pots around the house. He's a wiz at it."

"Really?" The scientist in me is interested. "Is there a special trick to it?"

"Orchids are epiphytes," Lester says. "They can only live on other objects, like rough bark or stone, and they need very specific conditions to thrive." Seeing my expression, he adds, "It sounds hard, I guess, but if you just know what they need and give it to them, they respond and make the most extraordinary blossoms!" He grins at me as he reaches for a third sample.

A little *ping* goes off in my head. He's a kind man. A soon-to-be unmarried man. A man who makes fragile, dependent creatures bloom. My hopes rise like a thousand helium balloons.

"You should come back here before the wedding. Then Mom could show you some sample frosting orchids instead of sending photos."

Lester looks at Jessica. "We hadn't planned on it."

I improvise. "I think it would be a good idea. Those photos don't always come out well, and you could spend some time on the island and get recommendations for things your guests can do while they're here."

Jessica startles me by standing and grabbing up the empty sample tray. "Let me help you clean up." She zooms off to the kitchen, leaving me no choice but to follow.

"You're trying to set them up!" she says once we're out of earshot. She has pale eyes with blonde lashes and doesn't wear any make-up at all that I can tell. Standing in my kitchen with her fists on her thin little hips, she looks me up and down.

"Me?" I try to act innocent, but can see that won't work. "They seemed to hit it off. Don't you think they look good together?"

"*Maybe.*" Jessica continues to check me out.

What am I trying to do here? Palm my problem off on someone else? Well … yes. But Lester *likes* her. I'm sure of it. Maybe he'd know how to handle Mom, bring out the best in her.

"They might enjoy each other. Why should they be alone if they don't have to be?"

She looks unconvinced. "It's just …my dad's a really special guy."

Good. My mom *needs* a really special guy.

And Lester's a big boy. He can make his own decisions.

I think fast.

"I'm sorry your fiancé couldn't come. How about I make you a box of samples to take home to him?"

"He'd love that. Thank you!" Then she catches herself and frowns. "I still know what you're doing!"

"Why shouldn't your dad come out another time? What harm would it do?" When she hesitates, I keep talking. "You'll be married soon, and he'll be on his own."

"I know he's lonely," she admits.

I wait.

"I suppose it wouldn't hurt to ask him about it."

Chapter Eighteen

I don't know what Jeremy wants from me. Although he finds a way to see me almost every day and gives me long, soulful looks, he shows no signs of wanting to hold my hand or kiss me. On top of that, I saw a photo of a girl in his wallet the other day when we got ice cream at The Super Scoop.

Do I want him to kiss me? Yes, but I don't think I'll have a choice. It seems like I'm good for hiking and diving, but I'm not the kind of girl boys want to kiss.

Dizzy gives Jeremy a shift within a few days of his arrival. He's an instant hit with the customers, wearing four or five of Dizzy's buttons at a time, remembering the names of returning diners, and cracking jokes as he carries out armfuls of lunch specials, never dropping a thing. He also juggles and keeps threatening to sing karaoke.

"How'd you learn to do all this?" I ask him.

"I dunno. I must have done it in a past life."

When Jeremy calls me to find out where to get the Sunday Los Angeles Times, I tell him, "Meet me at Island Lil's at eight o'clock Sunday morning," then have to scramble to fit our meeting into a busy three-cake day.

"The van's packed," I tell Mom. "I just need to drop you at Channel Island at 7:30. I'll be back to get you by 10:00." I'll do the other two cakes myself in the afternoon, both for evening weddings.

"Big date?" she asks, raising an eyebrow.

Mom must have noticed that, to go get the Sunday paper, I've put on one of my few cute outfits—a pair of short-shorts and a little top— and let my hair fall in a long cascade down my back. I figure, just in case the girl in Jeremy's wallet is a long lost cousin, it wouldn't hurt to be prepared.

"Maybe," I say. My spirits lift. I put on some lip gloss, feeling pretty.

"I wouldn't get my hopes up. He's just killing time with you." She tosses off the remark as if she's saying it's going to rain, while putting fruit in the blender for her breakfast smoothie.

Somewhere inside me, a tiny hairline crack appears, then widens and tears open, leaving me shaking. As my anger grows into rage, I can almost feel the heat rising off my body, like steam from molten lava.

"Why are you like this?" The words burst out of me.

Mom stops the blender, eyes wide. "Like what?" If I'd sprouted horns she couldn't look more surprised.

"Don't you want me to be happy? Why do you always shoot me down?" I'm yelling now, not caring how far my voice might carry. "Just stop it, okay?!"

I want to make a dramatic exit, but I have to drive Mom to the Channel Island resort. As quickly as I erupted, I rein myself in. "I'll be out in the van." I stalk out with as much dignity as I can muster.

A few minutes later, Mom and I make our trip in silence. As we pull up, she starts to open her door, then turns back.

"I didn't mean to upset you," she says in a tiny voice.

When I don't respond, she leaves, and I go to meet Jeremy.

• • •

He waits on a bench outside Island Lil's with coffee for both of us. I sit beside him, steaming, my insides doing somersaults. He gives me a long look.

"You okay?" He hands me a cup, then puts his hand on my shoulder. It's warm from the cup.

I nod. We sit on the bench, sipping. After a few minutes, Javier Hernandez rolls up in his battered pick-up, the bed filled with copies of the Sunday Times. He sells the papers right out of the back, arriving every Sunday in his straw hat, a feather tucked into the band.

"This is awesome!" Jeremy buys a paper, and we spread it out, reading and enjoying the sun. I can see that Jeremy's holding off his questions, not wanting to upset me further.

The usual group of guys is hanging out across the street in front of the pharmacy, which has nice benches. People come and go, getting their papers. A fellow with a huge pot-belly rolls up on his skateboard. He gets his coffee at Lil's and rolls away, sipping as he goes.

Slowly, I start to relax. I stretch out my legs in the sun, handing Jeremy the Business section, while I take the Calendar. A shadow falls across my legs. I know without even looking up that it's Zack.

He wears a tank top, jeans, and a bandana around his forehead. He stands there, his eyes on me, taking in my hot little shorts and flowing hair.

"Hey, Alex," he says. His smile's so warm that I begin a slow melt, despite everything – my fight with Mom and his being Rosie's boyfriend now.

"Hey, Zack." After a minute, I remember Jeremy. "Zack, this is Jeremy Broadman." I enunciate "Broadman," to be sure Zack gets exactly who I'm hanging with these days.

"H'lo there!" Jeremy, sprawling next to me on our bench in the sun, peers over the edge of his paper, then sits up abruptly.

"Hey." Zack stands very straight, checking Jeremy out and not even pretending to look friendly about it. I can tell they recognize each other from the night of the wedding, when Zack took me home instead of Jeremy.

"How long you out here for?" Zack asks.

"Seven more weeks."

Zack bites his lip.

"I'm working at Dizzy's," Jeremy offers. "I was lucky and got a regular part-time shift."

Zack bites his lip some more.

"What do you guys do round here? For entertainment?" Jeremy asks.

"Lotsa things," Zack says, straight-faced. "Feed the wild cats. Go down to the pier and drop rocks in the water."

Jeremy doesn't miss a beat. "I'll have to try those. After I've read all of Dizzy's buttons." He turns to me. "I wanna learn how to dive."

"Seriously? You should take a certification class at Nate's Dive Shop. Then we can go together," I tell him.

Zack's eyes light up. As far as diving skills go, we both know Jeremy doesn't stand a chance against him. "Sure," he says. "You guys can come out on Kap's boat. I'll take you down." Then he throws down his challenge. "If you're up for it."

"I'm up for it," Jeremy snaps back.

Omigod. I'm going diving again.

• • •

Once again, Mom forgets to place an order with our wholesale supplier.

"Honey, would you please go pick up what we need at Henderson's groceries?" She's been polite and careful with me ever since I yelled at her.

I stare at her. Paying retail island prices for our entire weekly ingredient order—is she kidding? At the crazy-low prices we charge, we'll be paying people for the privilege of making their cakes. Even I know this, and I'm only seventeen.

Shaken, I don't go to Henderson's, but instead place a special rush order with our wholesaler and wheedle him to waive the extra fee.

"We can't afford it!" I tell him. "And look at all the business we give you!"

He groans. "Okay, but only because I like you, Alex."

I hang up with him and go find Mom. "Hey, you mind if I order the supplies myself for a while? It would be a good learning experience."

"Sure, but just let me check your orders in advance, so I can be sure everything's right," Mom says, putting on her most official tone.

"Okay." I know I won't do it, and she'll forget all about it. Ordering the supplies myself will be a lot more work, but we'll cut our costs and maybe make some money. I keep thinking about how well we'd do if we raised our prices. I decide to sit down and crunch some numbers that evening.

While I'm at it, I look up a phone number. Then I hesitate to call. Do I really want to inflict Mom's craziness on the nice Lester Lindstrom? The thing is, they liked each other. There was something between them—a spark.

I start to call him, then hang up. I have to do this right. I call Jessica.

"He thinks your mom's really pretty and talented," she reports. "But it's hard for me to get away. My fiancé's working weekends to pay for the honeymoon, and we hate being apart."

I just happen to have a solution to her problem. "Why don't you stay in town with him then? We'll take good care of your dad."

I can feel her wavering. "It would be nice for us to have some time alone. And honestly, I think Dad would like to go."

A day later, it's settled. Lester's coming out for the weekend. By himself. He'll arrive Saturday morning, with an appointment to preview the sample orchids at one, and will stay the night at the Seashell Hotel down the street from us.

I plot ways to give him and Mom as much time as possible alone together. I ease a fourteen-inch double chocolate chip layer out of its pan, laying it to rest on a cooling rack. "Mom, I've got to help Dizzy with some stuff Saturday afternoon. You handle Lester, okay?"

Mom pushes a strand of hair out of her eyes with her forearm and hands me the next pan from the oven. "I don't know why he had to come out here. I could have emailed him some photos."

"Maybe he likes it here. Maybe you could show him around after your meeting." I wiggle my eyebrows up and down at her in a meaningful way. "Get to know him."

She throws down a potholder on the counter. "Alexandra! He's married!"

"Separated. As in, practically divorced."

Mom tries to look stern, but a smile fights its way to the surface. "He's not my type!"

Of course he isn't. He's nice and has a good job. I slip a second layer onto the cooling rack, the rich scent of chocolate curling its way into my brain. "You barely know him. But he seems like a good guy— and successful, too!"

In an instant, Mom's eyes turns dark with doubt. "Do you think he'd like me?" With her finger, she traces a line in some flour on the counter.

"Of course! Why wouldn't he?"

She pushes out a deep sigh. I soften at the sight of her vulnerable expression.

I pick up a towel and dab some flour off her nose. "His daughter said you impressed him."

"Really?"

"I even know what you should wear to go out to dinner."

"Dinner!"

But I'm already moving her down the hallway to her bedroom, where I pull from the closet a dress I've always liked on her. It's softly romantic, in a floral print of pale greens, pinks and lavenders.

"That old thing?" Mom sniffs.

"It makes you look beautiful. And if you put your hair up and let little curls fall down in the front?" I hold the dress up to her body. "He'll flip over you!"

"Well, I guess it *is* flattering, isn't it?" Mom looks at the dress with a thoughtful expression. "And with my lavender eye shadow!"

We plan what Mom'll show Lester of the island during the day and where they'll go to dinner. "La Petite Paris," she says. "That's perfect for a classy date. And then we can stroll along the Seawalk afterward."

After she's gone to bed, I'm too excited to sleep. Maybe all Mom needs is to be happy again. And then I can be happy, too. I lie awake for a long time, my head full of hopes and possibilities.

When I finally fall asleep, I dream that I'm diving with Zack in an enormous cathedral of billowing kelp, but nothing grabs or entangles me. Nothing's holding me back.

• • •

Roy's wife greets me at their front door, her face and arms tan from two weeks in the sun. There's something in her hair that might be peanut butter, but I can't be sure.

"Hi, Cindy. How'd your trip go?"

"Great! We put floaties on the boys and threw them into every body of water we could find." She shows me to their back yard swing set, where Roy's pushing their kids, ages three and five, who are seated on separate swings and yelling "Higher! Higher!"

"And. Now. I. Will. Deactivate. Your. Brains." Roy says in a high, robotic voice.

"Dad's an alien, Mom," says the older boy. "And we're astronauts."

"Astronauts whose lunch is ready. Your daddy needs to talk to Alex, so come on in and wash your hands."

Left alone together, Roy and I sit down on the swings the boys left behind.

"I feel bad about what happened, Alex. I should have realized you'd have a problem with your mom and given you more support." Together, we push off with our feet and start to swing.

"It's okay. I'm sorry I messed everything up. But I still wanna design a research project."

We pump our legs, pushing our swings higher as we talk.

"How will you fund it?"

"I got a little bit saved up," I say, thinking of the diving equipment stashed at Jenna and Dizzy's.

He flies past me backward as I go forward. "Aim for a write-up in *Teen Science Journal*. It'll open up your chances for scholarships."

We go sit at the picnic table so I can describe my research ideas to him. He peppers me with questions until we eventually choose a topic.

"This sounds great, Alex! Now you just need to make a detailed research plan. To get into *Teen Science Journal*, you're going to have to be really thorough." We go over the components needed for the plan.

I sigh, thinking of the class I'm going to miss. "They don't like me at Beach City College anymore, do they?"

"I'm sure they'd still be glad to have you, Alex, but you know you want a top program."

"But, my mom…"

"Alex, you're a good daughter. You want to stand by your mom. But don't sell yourself short either."

Cindy comes out and stands, watching us, her hands on her hips. "Do you two kids want lunch?"

"We sure do!" Roy answers, and I second that. I'm starving.

• • •

Jeremy and I sit on a bench out on the Seawalk talking. We've gotten in the habit of coming here almost every evening for a least a little while. The dark harbor's filled with the twinkling lights of boats, each a small floating home. Tourists stroll past on their way to dinner or holding giant waffle cones of ice cream from The Super Scoop. There's no one here I know, besides Jeremy. The Seawalk in the summertime might as well have a sign on it, saying "Visitors Only."

"So is it love?" he asks. "Between Sue and Lester?"

"Could be." I can still hardly believe it. Lester and Mom have been on the phone every day since his trip out here, and he's got plans to come again next week.

"He's good for her," I tell him. "He doesn't take crap from her. When she's with me, she won't listen and then she either shuts down or gets really mad."

He raises an eyebrow. "Ah, yes. I know someone with a temper. Although she'd call it an anger management problem."

"Who's that?" I ask him, hoping he'll open up a bit. Jeremy has this way of getting you to talk about yourself, while spilling very little on his own life.

"My girlfriend," he says.

So he does have a girlfriend. I remember the photo of an icy looking blonde holding a tennis racket.

"Is that the girl in your wallet?"

"Yeah. Although I'm going to Stanford, and she's going to UCLA, so it's hard to say anymore."

"Whether she's in your wallet?"

"Whether she's going to keep being my girlfriend." Jeremy rolls his eyes. "You know what I mean."

"Actually, I don't." As I recall, she was really pretty in the photo, even though she looked like the sort of person who would snap her fingers at me and say "You, over there!" to get my attention.

Be fair. You don't even know her.

"Well, let's just say," he chooses his words carefully, "that things are complicated. And this summer we're living three thousand miles apart."

She doesn't sound like much of a girlfriend to me. I don't understand why Jeremy would carry her photo around with him. But there seem to be a lot of things about boys that I don't understand.

In the distance a giant cruise ship appears, headed for Paradise Harbor, where it will moor overnight and all day tomorrow, disgorging its passengers into our bars, restaurants, and trinket shops. "My ship has come in!" Dizzy likes to say whenever one of the behemoths arrives with its hordes of money-spending vacationers.

"So where's your girlfriend this summer?"

"In New York. She got an internship with an ad agency."

I still can't believe how Jeremy can speak of these things so casually, as if of course everyone goes to schools like Stanford and UCLA, and everyone has great jobs in New York City. He must see something on my face.

"What?"

"Well, you make it seem so normal. You know, traveling, and getting interesting jobs. Going to college."

"But you're going to college, right? You travel."

"No." My throat and eyes burn. I turn away so he can't see my face.

Jeremy pulls himself from his habitual slouch. "Oh, come on. You've traveled somewhere."

"No."

"What, were you raised by wolves?"

"It's my mom." I can't keep the bitterness out of my voice. "I think she just wants me to grow roots into the soil here, like a tree."

"Well, you've gone away on vacation, right?"

I shake my head.

"For a weekend?"

"Nope."

We sit there for a moment on our bench. I'm in a corner, knees up with my arms wrapped around them. Until a moment ago, Jeremy was spread over the rest of our bench, but now he's sitting up straight. He points a finger at me. "Listen to me. You're taking a couple of days off. We're going into town."

Go to Los Angeles with Jeremy? I think fast. I would die to go. But it would cost a lot. And what does he expect from me? "What is this, Jeremy? A sleepover?"

He assumes an innocent expression. "Hey, I told you about Jennifer. My intentions are honorable."

Jeremy and Jennifer. It's too cute. "Where would we sleep?"

"In a hotel." He gives me a bland look.

"I don't *think* so. Or if we do, you're on the floor."

"Separate rooms. Scout's honor." He tries to give me the Boy Scouts' signal, but not knowing exactly how it goes, ends up flashing me a peace sign.

"Two hotel rooms?" I don't want to tell him how poor I am. "How much will it cost?"

"Nothing."

"Come on!"

"No, listen," Jeremy says. "This one's on me."

"I can't do that!"

"Yes, you can. I accept your acts of friendship every day. You can accept one of mine."

Still I hesitate. I'm dying to go. And I have the Broadmans' diving equipment to sell. And the money from Nate's job.

But I also have to fund my research project. I run a quick calculation in my head.

"I'm going to pay our round trip fares on the Traveler," I tell him. "Let me at least do that much."

"Done."

"And we'll have separate rooms, like you said." I attempt to give him a stern look. "Just so you don't try anything."

But, maybe I'd want him to, if he were available. Too bad he has a girlfriend. I'm sick of being a goody-goody. Little, cringing, obedient, under-her-mama's-thumb Alexandra. Little, perfect please-the-grownups Alexandra. I'm a bore. I want to get drunk, make out with a boy, maybe do more than that. But it can't be with Jeremy.

Where can we go for only two days? I want to go to someplace exotic and fantastic and far away.

"Jeremy, where are we going?"

114

"Somewhere every kid should go," he says. "We're going to Disneyland."

Chapter Nineteen

"You want to leave the island with that boy?" Mom paces across the living room, then whirls. "Alexandra, is there something I should know about you and him? And what about your responsibilities here?"

I make myself speak calmly. "First off, we're just friends, and we're getting separate rooms. Second, we're going during the week, when it's quiet. It won't interfere with our schedule."

She dissolves into tears, which used to work on me when I was younger. Now I just give her a stony glare.

"This boy's...." She stops herself, but dabs at her eyes with a tissue. "I just want to protect you from getting hurt."

I don't see how Jeremy could ever hurt me more than my mother has. "Mom, I'm going. And I have it all figured out. I'll make all the layers for the weekend before I leave. And I'll order supplies. You'll just need to pick up the supplies on Thursday and take the layers out of the freezer Friday morning."

Her face goes redder as her voice gets huffy. "Don't treat me like an imbecile. I started this business when you were still in diapers!"

"Then take responsibility for it!"

She flinches as if I'd struck her. "I can't allow you to go on this trip."

"I'm not asking your permission. It's all organized. Jeremy and I are going to Disneyland. That's it."

"Well, don't expect me to help you pay for this!"

She stomps away, while I think to myself *yes*. Even if it's just for two days, I'm free.

• • •

I never realized how much fun it is to look forward to a trip. And to shop for clothes with a bundle of cash in your hand.

I take some pieces of choice equipment down to Nate at the Dive Shop. He whistles when he sees the dive computers. "Nice!"

"I'll give you a discount if you give me cash."

He folds his long, skinny body onto a stool behind his counter. His sharp elbows look like they're about to drill through the counter top. Nate specializes in everchanging facial hair, currently a grizzled soul patch and before that a goatee.

"Nah, it's okay," he says, handing me the full amount in crisp green bills.

I guess he's gone soft after watching me scrub toilets for years.

Even if Jeremy does have a girlfriend, this is still not the weekend for my old sweat pants. For Disneyland itself, I want skinny jeans, a cute top, and—my only concession to practicality—comfortable sneakers. Jeremy has said to bring a bathing suit and something to wear out to dinner. Separate rooms or not, I'm going to look good.

At Maureen's Fashion Hut, Maureen herself helps me find the perfect black jeans and two tops that fit exactly right. I bypass their one-piece women's racing suits. I have a half dozen of those at home—the ones that make your shoulders resemble an NFL quarterback's. Instead Maureen brings me a choice of cute bikinis, and I throw two onto my pile of purchases. Next, a fitted dress that catches the peach and pink of my skin, for when Jeremy and I go out to dinner.

I'm heading for the cash register when I see the matching bra and panty sets in aqua and lavender, with bits of lace trim. I stop.

I've never worn anything in my life but functional white cotton bras and briefs.

"Aren't they yummy?" Maureen says.

I've always admired the way she looks so perfect and put together. This morning, her eyelashes stand out in little spikes around her eyes and a thin gold chain trickles down and ends in a pendant just above a faint shadow of cleavage.

I hesitate.

"Oh, go on!" She winks. "Pretty underwear puts a girl in touch with her own power."

I snap up one set in each color. Somewhere, among the wet suits and gym shorts, I'll make room in my wardrobe for clothes that are flirty and sexy. And also room in my life for the changes that go with them.

• • •

We're scheduled for the seven am Traveler from Paradise to Long Beach. Evelyn drives Jeremy down into town to pick me up, then takes Carousel Avenue from the center of town to the boat terminal. If she disapproves of our little overnight expedition, she's keeping it to herself.

We drive past a row of shops on our right: bicycle and golf cart rentals along with places that sell hats, sunglasses, ceramics by local artists, postcards, and kitty cats made out of sea shells. On our left, the Seawalk meanders along the edge of the water. Looking back, we can see all of Paradise Cove, with its town and harbor.

Evelyn leaves us on the curb outside the terminal with our bags. I'm in my skinny jeans, an off-the-shoulder blouse, and pretty sandals.

As I fling my bag over my shoulder, Rosie speeds past in a golf cart, Zack in the passenger seat. From the corner of my eye, I see his head start to turn as the cart goes by. When his head can't turn any further, his whole body turns until he's facing backward, all to keep sight of me, leaving the island in a hot outfit with Jeremy Broadman and an overnight bag.

I swallow a giggle. *Take that, Zack Attack.* As Zack's eyes bore holes into me and we walk onto the boat, I feel Jeremy put a hand on the small of my back.

• • •

I try not to gawk as I stand in the lobby of our hotel. Jeremy's checking us in, standing at the front desk with his back to me. On the table in the center is an arrangement of flowers and branches that could house a colony of baboons. I reach out and touch a petal. They're real.

Something scratches the corner of my mind. I should call Mom to make sure she remembers to pick up the supplies today.

No calls, I remind myself. It's enough that I left two notes, one on the kitchen counter, and one taped to her bathroom mirror.

As Jeremy walks up to me, I pull out my cell and hand it to him. "Keep this for me, okay? Don't let me call Mom."

"Happy to." He pockets it.

Jeremy has gotten us adjoining rooms connected by a door that, he points out in a dry tone, I can dead bolt at any time if I feel it necessary.

"I'll keep that in mind," I tell him.

The hotel rooms are so beautiful that I could just stay here. I don't even need to go to Disneyland. The sheets are crisp and expensive-feeling, and the carpet's thick, with not even one stain anywhere. There's a bucket that you can fill with your own ice and a refrigerator stocked with candy bars and cookies and nuts.

I want to savor every moment. I touch one of the pillows on the bed. It's the softest thing I've ever felt. Our pillows at home are these hard foam things. I sit on the bed for a few minutes, hugging the pillow and taking in the bedspread, the rug, the wallpaper. The colors and patterns match perfectly, as if everything was bought new and at the same time.

Best of all is the bathroom, with a mirror that lights up and shows you every single pore and blemish on your face, a hair dryer, a white terry bath robe and slippers, and—my favorite—a basket full of free things you can take home. I sit down on the edge of the bathtub looking at my loot. There's a sewing kit, shampoo and conditioner, lotion, and something to shine your shoes with.

"Alex?" Jeremy's voice calls from the connecting door to our bedrooms.

"Come in!"

When his head appears around the edge of the bathroom door, he smiles to see me smelling the lotion and trying it on my hand.

"Don't poke fun," I say.

"I wouldn't think of it. You ready to go?"

Am I ever.

• • •

I'm nine again, except that when I was really nine I never went to Disneyland. Rather, I was reading *Anne of Green Gables* and doing sixth grade math while Mom taught me the fine points of a fondant icing.

We're at Splash Mountain.

"Do you mind getting wet?" Jeremy asks me, then remembers who he's speaking to. I climb into a car designed to resemble a log and sit beside him, leaning forward in excitement. Seated, we inch our way up an incline, reach the top, cross a short flat area, then fall forty feet, while we all scream and close our eyes against the spray of water around us.

I want to store up this day and keep it forever, so I never forget a moment. "Let's do all the fast rides!" We do. Space Mountain, Star Tours, the Matterhorn, and Big Thunder Mountain Railroad. I have so much fun, I only think of Mom once.

"Each one has its own different style!" I love Thunder Mountain, with its bumps and dips and that steep clickety-clack climb, and the Matterhorn, which takes you through a well of blackness then hurtles you into the light and through a series of curves.

At first, Jeremy laughs with pleasure at my enthusiasm, but after half a dozen rollercoaster rides, he's got a green tinge. "How about something more mellow?"

"Okay!" I'm happy to do anything here. But the thing I love most of all is Peter Pan's Flight. I hang over the edge of our airborne car, breathless, looking down at the tops of skyscrapers, a tiny mountain peak below, and the many twinkling lights of a city, viewed from the air at night.

"It's so beautiful!" I tell Jeremy. "Is that what it's really like?"

"What?"

"Flying. In a plane. At night," I say. "Is that what it looks like?"

I can sense his astonishment, even though he keeps his face expressionless. My ears turn warm. How embarrassing to be such a total rube.

"Yeah," he says. "That's what it's like."

Finally, we take a break. I fall onto a bench and reach for my cell phone, only to remember that Jeremy has it. What's Mom doing now? Did she get the supplies?

"Jeremy, I'm getting this urge to call her."

He flops down next to me. "Resist. I promise you. She's fine."

I remember what Zack always used to say. "Do you think I baby her?"

Jeremy waves at Donald Duck as he passes by. "I think she's got a good thing going, having you around. Let's do Pirates of the Caribbean! That's an easy one."

I love everything: the rides, the lights, the characters in their costumes, the music. I love sitting next to Jeremy and yelling like lunatics through the fast parts. I love the Sleeping Beauty Castle and Minnie Mouse and the Enchanted Tiki Room. And I love it all the more because I'm not sure I'll ever be back here again.

• • •

At the hotel, we shower and dress in our separate spaces, getting ready for dinner, after which I hear a knock on the door connecting our rooms. Jeremy's looking good in a simple blue shirt, tan slacks, and loafers. Even I can tell his clothes are beautifully cut and fit him perfectly. I smooth my hands down the skirt of my inexpensive cotton dress, which seemed so nice in the store. I hope it's okay.

"You look great." He answers my unspoken question. His eyes tell me he means it, too, which sends my confidence spiraling upward.

"Thanks. So do you!"

He clears his throat, his cheeks reddening. "There's a nice restaurant upstairs with a view. I thought we'd go there."

I know from reading the Guest Information Book in my room that it's a four star restaurant. "That sounds good," I say casually. Jeremy doesn't have to know that my only brush with fine dining was a trip to El Matador in Long Beach, which has velvet flocked wallpaper, an all-you-can-eat salad buffet, and early bird specials beginning at 4:30.

Our table at the restaurant has a white tablecloth and groans with plates and glassware and silverware, way more than you would ever need for one meal. Then, before we even order, a guy comes and takes away some of it, which seems to indicate they've caught their mistake.

I ask him how his grandparents are doing. "You've got such an awesome family." People flit around us filling water glasses, bringing bread and butter and menus, checking in to make sure we're happy and comfortable. Like the glassware, there seem to be a lot more people around than strictly necessary.

Jeremy has a strange expression on his face. "They're good folks. But it's not always that easy to be a Broadman."

"What do you mean?"

"I mean, you have to be a certain way, and if you're not, you don't fit in."

"I didn't notice that."

"Wait till you get to know us!" He dives into his menu, which has just arrived.

When I first see the prices here, I think I'm reading them wrong. I squint at them in disbelief and then peek out from the side of the menu to see if Jeremy wants to make a run for the all-night diner down the street. But he just asks the waiter about one of the specials.

Burgundy Escargots en Croute, Perigueux Truffled Lobster Thermidor —my head's swimming. But since Jeremy got to ask questions, it seems like I can, too.

"Excuse me, how is the filet of sole prepared?" I pipe up bravely when it's my turn. Jeremy hides a smile, which makes me even more determined to hold up my end of the conversation. I manage to place my order, then stick my tongue out at him after the waiter's gone. He laughs outright.

The meal's delicious, but best of all is the triple chocolate threat that arrives for dessert. As I taste the first bite, I close my eyes. "I'm in heaven, Jeremy." I wanted to share a dessert, but Jeremy insisted I get my own. Now I'm glad he did.

"Thank you," I tell him. "I'll always remember this day."

As we ride down the elevator toward our rooms, I find my palms getting clammy. Don't be ridiculous, I tell myself. We've already agreed we're just friends. To stop my racing mind I blurt, "So do you have plans to see Jennifer this summer?"

"I dunno," Jeremy says. We're in the hallway now, letting ourselves into his bedroom. He shrugs. "The last time we saw each other was kind of rough. We weren't exactly getting along."

"Why not?"

"It's not easy for me to talk about." Jeremy walks over to the window.

"Oh. Well, how did you meet her then?"

"She's my sister, Emma's, best friend. We kind of drifted into this thing together." All of a sudden, Jeremy seems to be speaking from a place deep inside of him. A place that's dark and painful.

"But you don't have anything in common with Emma, right?" Caught up in what he's saying, I forget to be nervous. I curl into an armchair, slipping off my sandals and pulling my legs under me.

Jeremy gives me a philosophical little smile, "No, but Jennifer's the kind of girl my family would expect me to date."

Jeremy has somehow morphed from my easy-going, comfortable friend into an attractive, mysterious stranger. I shift in my chair, putting my feet down and crossing my legs. I notice again the way his hair flows back from his forehead. His shirt's made of soft, expensive looking fabric that I want to touch.

What's wrong with me? I keep wondering how it would feel to kiss Jeremy. It seems like he's getting more and more uncomfortable, now pacing around the room. I start to say something, then stop, then start again. "So, I guess you and Jennifer are on the rocks?"

"It's hard to say what we are." Jeremy sits down, then, as if he's too restless to stay in one place, immediately jumps to his feet. "It's only ten thirty. You want to go down to the pool?"

Chapter Twenty

At this hour, the pool's deserted. I drift on my back, patting the surface of the water with my hands. As I look up into the sky, tops of palm trees sway into the edges of my vision. Jeremy's been doing laps, but now pops up next to me, his hair slicked back like the dark head of a seal.

"Hot tub, mademoiselle? I'll race you."

"You're on!"

He has the advantage of being pointed in the right direction. I flip in the water and race after him down the long pool. He's a better swimmer than I expected, but I was born part sea otter. I catch up to him, my arms and legs strong and supple as they drive me forward. A few more powerful kicks and I touch the wall a fingertip ahead of Jeremy.

"Aw, man! A little thing like you?" Jeremy smacks the water. "I demand a rematch!"

"Oh, so you like punishment?"

"Don't worry about me!" Jeremy sounds exasperated, as if he'd thought beating me was a no brainer.

We position ourselves with our feet against the short wall of the shallow end, one hand gripping the pool edge.

"Ready, set, go!"

We launch ourselves at the same moment. Forward. I focus on the thought, my hands slicing through the water, my legs and feet propelling me ahead. I reach the wall a second before Jeremy does.

"Victory!" I raise my arms, my fingers in two "Vs."

He shakes his head. "Now I think you were raised by dolphins."

We pull ourselves out of the pool. Water drips from the ends of Jeremy's board shorts, which come down to his knees. I find myself looking at his chest and arms. Suddenly conscious of my bikini and how little it covers, I hustle across to the tub and get in.

It's my first time ever in a hot tub. It's delicious—steaming and bubbly. We sit there in a contented silence, our heads sticking out of the water.

"I love this," I say. "It's like sitting in club soda."

Affection blooms on Jeremy's face. "It's fun to take you places. You're so innocent."

"Yeah, I'm good for a laugh." I feel another flash of embarrassment. There I go again, being a hick.

Jeremy grins. "Hold on." He jumps out and crosses over to a wall where he pushes a button. The jets of water streaming from the sides of the tub kick into high gear, churning the surface. We pull up our feet and bob, letting the jets move us around. We bump into each other as we float.

"Bumper cars!" I hit him with my hip.

He pushes off from the side, drifting into me with his shoulder. "Oops! Excuse me!" he says. He bumps into me again.

I push him away, but his arm goes around my waist, and all of a sudden his face is right there, and his eyes are like crystals split into a million facets of different blues. He looks down at me with the most tender expression on his face.

"Alex, you're so awesome." And then, he kisses me.

We kiss for a long moment while I wonder how I'm supposed to feel. His lips are soft. His heart beats a slow, steady rhythm and his arms curl around me, warm and protective. It's all very safe and comfortable and Jeremy-like.

He pulls his arms back, shaking his head and moving away from me. "That was wrong. I shouldn't have done that."

I swallow hard and turn my back on him, feeling abandoned and ridiculous. I guess he didn't like kissing me.

On the other hand, I'm not sure I liked kissing him either. I mean, it wasn't bad. But it wasn't sexy and exciting and *omigod*, like kissing Zack was.

Still, he's the second guy who hasn't wanted me this summer. Zack doesn't want me. Jeremy doesn't want me. I feel him move up behind me.

"I'm really sorry," he says. "I totally blew it."

I turn to face him. "It's not your fault. I guess I'm just not attractive," I say. "You know, to guys."

Jeremy looks incredulous. "Are you *kidding?* You're *hot!*"

I know he's just saying that to be nice.

"C'mon, let's get outta here before we boil." He pulls me out of the hot tub and takes me up to our rooms.

"Now listen to me," he says, once we're inside. "Do you have any idea how amazing you are?"

"No." I'm drenched and forlorn, standing in the middle of Jeremy's room with my towel wrapped around me.

"Any guy would want you. You're a sweet, beautiful, flame-haired, heroic ninja warrior goddess, that's what you are. I would take you in a second. But …," he stops for a long moment, "I'm in a really weird place right now. With Jennifer, and with my life." He turns to face me, looking nervous and vulnerable in a way that I've never seen him. "You're just gonna have to trust me. This isn't about you."

"I'm sorry you wasted your time, bringing me to Disneyland."

"I didn't waste my time." He's shaking his head. "I told you before. You're awesome. I knew you would be."

"Really?" I sniffle a little, starting to feel hopeful, while he grins at me reassuringly.

"Trust me," he says again. "There's no one I'd rather be here with than you."

• • •

We stay up talking until three in the morning, when I finally stumble off to bed in my own room. After we wake up, Jeremy orders a huge room service breakfast that's delivered on its own table, with a giant pot of coffee and orange juice and silver domes covering all the food. I pick up each dome, examining what's underneath. "Look, Jeremy. The butter has its own little dome!"

"You don't say!" He hands me my orange juice, which is in another one of those stemmed glasses. "It's weird," he says, "I just have this funny feeling."

"That what?"

"That we'll always be friends."

A warm glow starts in my chest and radiates through the rest of me. "I'd like that."

"A toast!" He raises his glass. "To Sue-avoidance! And moving on with your life!"

"And hot tubs!" I say.

"And escaping your past!"

"And triple chocolate threat!" I feel drunk, not on alcohol, but on pleasure and independence.

"And beautiful mermaid-girls! And friendship!"

We touch our glasses together and drink our juice.

• • •

We board the Traveler at three o'clock that afternoon wearing identical Disneyland t-shirts that Jeremy insisted on buying. In my backpack are a bag of salt water taffy and a stuffed Eeyore, also gifts from Jeremy. It's been a bittersweet two days—having so much fun, yet realizing at the same time that guys just don't think of me as girlfriend material. No matter what I say or do or wear, I'm destined to be the girl-next-door, the sidekick.

We settle into our seats as the big catamaran powers out of Long Beach Harbor. It's a one-hour boat ride. Jeremy reads the paper, while I rest my head against the back of my seat and close my eyes. I didn't call my mother once in two days. It feels wonderful, but at the same time, worry nags at me.

All Mom had to do was pick up the supplies yesterday and take the cake layers out of the freezer today. She can remember that much, I tell myself, especially since I left reminder notes.

I only got four hours sleep last night. Lulled by the boat's motor and the rocking of the waves, I doze.

• • •

I wake up with a start, Jeremy's hand on my shoulder. He's shaking it. "Wake up, Alex! Now!"

Squinting, I look around. The thrum of the motor has stopped. Since we're not moving forward, the boat rises and falls with the ocean, tipping from side to side. A woman cries out as a passenger loses his balance and almost falls. To my right, people cluster with their backs to me, looking out the boat's starboard windows.

Jeremy pulls me to my feet. "We're just outside Paradise Harbor. They're not letting us dock," he says.

"Why not?"

He draws me through the crowd to a window. I gasp, my heart sinking into my toes.

A plume of smoke rises ahead of me. There's a fire on the island.

Chapter Twenty-One

Mom. It's my first thought. Alone at home with our failing oven. But I'd already prepared the layers for the weekend, so she didn't have to bake while I was gone. It can't be our house. I take a deep breath.

A crackle, followed by the voice of one of the boat attendants over the speaker system. "We've been instructed to stand by. We'll be allowed to dock if and when they tell us the fire's contained."

I stare anxiously out the window. "It looks like the fire's in town," I say to Jeremy. My lips tremble. It's bad enough to have a fire in the unpopulated areas, but right in town? The houses are so close together. A whole block could go up in flames in a few minutes.

What about Zack, Jenna, and Dizzy? In a panic, I push my way through the crowd, looking for a boat attendant, Jeremy following me. I rush up to a guy in a Santa Rita Traveler uniform.

"When are we docking?"

"We're trying to get more information," he says, making a visible effort to sound patient. Passengers press up beside and around me, trying to hear what he's saying.

"Hey!" Jeremy barks at a big guy who has just muscled his way forward, knocking me sideways. *"Watch it!"* He puts an arm around me.

It's a windy day. I can tell because the boat rises in the air, lifted by an ocean swell, then plummets with a stomach-turning roll as the swell passes. It'd be a lot worse if we were further out to sea. My insides tie themselves into knots. Wind is bad news for firefighters.

The attendant is on a phone, asking questions, nodding his head. "Give me my cell phone!" I say to Jeremy. I should be able to get reception from here.

White-faced, he yanks it out and gives it to me. I try to call Mom but reach her voicemail. Checking messages, I find three from my mother, all from yesterday.

Message number one: "I picked up the supplies. My, those boxes are heavy!" Message number two: a whole carton of eggs arrived cracked.

The attendant speaks to all of us crowding around him. "The fire's under control, but an ambulance is on the scene." A rustle of fear runs through some of the people in the crowd.

Message number three from Mom, left last night. "Our Saturday morning client asked to change her lemon layers to coconut. I have to re-bake three layers tomorrow."

I go hot and cold all over. I think of our oven throwing out sparks, Zack's words: "That's dangerous," Mom there alone this morning, maybe even taking a nap while the layers baked.

I was so selfish. I could have paid to replace the oven.

"Where is it?" I lunge forward, grabbing the attendant's arm. "Where's the fire?"

He's still on the phone, reporting to us as he hears things.

"It started at a residence in town," he says to the crowd around him. "It didn't spread to neighboring homes, but there were injuries."

Please not our house. Please make Mom okay. "Where?" I press him. "Where in town was the fire?"

He consults over the phone again, nodding his head, then delivers his answer.

"Cinnamon Street."

• • •

Evelyn paces back and forth at the top of the gangplank, waiting for us. One look at her, and I know. "It's our house, isn't it?"

She nods. That's when it hits me. The only home I've ever had is on fire. My mother, the only family I've ever had, is in danger. The world breaks into a thousand fragments, forming and reforming into different images, like when you look through a kaleidoscope.

As we run for her golf cart, odd details catch my eye. Evelyn's fingernails painted into perfect dark cherries. A "Help Wanted" sign in the window of the waffle shop. A little girl in a bathing suit, her skinny arms in floaties. I don't understand how these normal things can still exist when my world is shattering into pieces around me.

"My mom? Is she okay?"

Panting, Evelyn says,"I don't know." She stomps the gas pedal to the floor, and the under-powered cart putt-putts off. Images in my head: my mother trapped, flames on her every side, the walls caving in. I lean forward, as if that will push the cart along. My nails bite into the palms of my hands. I focus on the pain; it's better than the gruesome thoughts I'm having.

The golf cart sputters along. "Can't this thing go any faster?" I'm frantic, almost whimpering.

"I'm trying." Evelyn, looking straight ahead, her shoulders hunched up around her ears, zooms through a stop sign without even slowing down.

I wheel around to Jeremy in the backseat. "Would it be faster if we ran?"

"I have to let you off here anyway," Evelyn says. We're three blocks from my house, and the street's jammed with people.

I jump from the cart while it's still moving, stumbling as my feet hit the ground. Jeremy and I try to run, but can't. We push our way through the crowds. More horrible images dance in front of my eyes—Mom completely alone, screaming for help, the exits blocked. I strain to see up the street, where my house is. Even more people block my path, along with a horde of flashing blue and red lights. The smoke burns my nose. As we near the house, I try again to run but trip and stub my toes on the huge fire hoses that snake along under our feet.

The boat guy said the fire was contained. Still, the smoke chokes me, filling my lungs. "Do you see anything?" My vision's blocked by the ocean of heads in front of us.

Jeremy's a lot taller than me. He scans the crowd. "Over there." He steers me toward a knot of firefighters working near their truck. Their faces, the only part of them not covered with heavy gear, are blackened from smoke, There's Darryl, along with some of the volunteers, Brady and a couple of other guys.

"Where's Mom? Is she okay?" I search their faces, looking for reassurance.

"They took her to the hospital. Smoke inhalation." Brady starts to add something, but I'm already pulling out my cell phone.

"I'll get Evelyn back. She'll take us."

We rush back the way we came and find Evelyn, who heads the golf cart for the hospital, taking corners like a race car driver. Mentally, I beat myself up. If I'd shared my money to replace that oven, none of this would have happened.

We reach the hospital admitting desk. "She's in Room Two," says the nurse on duty. I run to see her, afraid of what I'll find.

• • •

Mom leans back against the hospital pillows. Plastic tubes trail from her nose, accentuating the violet circles under her closed eyes. Her hands lie so still on the sheets that, for a moment, I think the worst. I catch my breath in a sob.

Her eyelids flutter.

"Oh, Mom!" I sit next to her and hold her hand. We sit there for a long time, quietly, while Jeremy waits outside, giving me time to be alone with her.

"I'm so sorry!"

Mom swallows with difficulty. Her eyes blink open for a minute, then close. The nurse comes in and tells me Mom will be fine in a day or so. "A neighbor got her out right away. She was really lucky."

I say a silent prayer of thanks — she's going to be okay. I'll do better from now on. I won't be so angry all the time. I'll be grateful for what I have.

"We'll replace the oven and fix the kitchen," I say to Mom. "Don't worry. We'll be up and running again soon."

She tries to say something. "Not the kitchen," she murmurs.

I lean closer. "What?"

"Candles. Fell asleep."

"Candles?" A low roar begins in my ears.

I can't believe it. I go away for less than forty-eight hours, and my crazy mother sets her bedroom on fire with some candles. I think of all the times I've warned her not to light candles and forget them. She could have burned down the entire town.

In a single moment, every hope I've ever had vanishes. She's a danger to herself and others. Lester will never marry a space queen like her. I see myself at age forty, living in Paradise, driving the wedding cake van, eating from takeout containers with my mother in our little living room.

She closes her eyes, while I contemplate my future. We'll never have enough. I'll have to take extra jobs just to get the rent paid. The children of people whose wedding cakes we've made will come to the island for their weddings, and we'll make their cakes too. I'll never dive again or marry. They'll bury me in my Sue's Wedding Cakery apron, a spatula in my hand.

"Alex." Mom puts her hand on mine. "I'm so sorry. You're a good girl."

"Just try to rest, okay?" We sit there, not speaking, holding hands, until she falls asleep.

• • •

Mom's bedroom and our bathroom are destroyed, the exterior walls and part of the roof gone, the fixtures and furniture blackened by smoke. The bed is charred beyond recognition. I look at it and shudder, thinking of what a close call it was.

JayBud Builders puts our repair job on rush status, giving us an estimate of $19,000 to repair the whole mess, plus install the new oven that I insist on. Because the fire was our fault, we have to pay for all the damages.

Expecting an explosion, I tell Mom about my ten thousand dollars. "The Broadmans—Jeremy's grandparents— gave it to me. I'm sorry I didn't tell you right away." For a minute, her eyes flash and her face darkens, and I think *here we go.* Just as suddenly, her expression changes, as if she has put on the emotional brakes. *"Well!"* she says. "That'll be a big help, won't it?"

But we're still nine thousand dollars short. Brady, who prepared the repair estimate for JayBud, says "Let me see what I can do." JayBud gives us a five thousand dollar discount, but we still have to raise four more thousand on our own.

"Things have a way of working out," Jenna says. She moves us in with her and Dizzy for the period of the construction, mom on their old futon and me in a sleeping bag on the floor. In keeping with Santa Rita tradition, a collection is organized. The folks in Paradise pull together when someone's having a tough time, chipping in with as few or many dollars as they can spare. I don't see how we can possibly get the thousands we need. But we do. Zack comes over two nights after the fire with a canvas bag that he holds up to us. "This should cover it." The bag is stuffed with bills and checks.

"You did this, Zack?" He looks so great, with his hair sticking out from his bandana, his world-class sexy arms and those wide shoulders that taper down so suddenly and disappear into that narrow waistband. I sigh to myself.

"Me and Dizzy," Zack says. "He made the phone calls and I went around and picked up the contributions." He empties the bag on the table. My eyes mist over when I see all those five and ten-dollar bills from folks who, like us, struggle to make ends meet. Zack hands me a long list of the people who gave cash, including Annabelle from the post office, the servers up at the Inn, Marlayne and Trish at the bank, and Roy. There are checks, too—from Nate's Dive Shop, Henderson's Groceries, Evelyn, and finally, one in a white envelope from Jeremy. It's for two thousand dollars and includes a note that simply says, "Please just take it."

"We have to write thank you notes," I say to Mom.

Brady shows up every day at the construction site with a double crew that works overtime to put our house back into shape in less than a week. In fact, it's better than before, because we have an all new bathroom, fresh paint throughout, and, at my insistence, a new oven.

I try to convince myself it's okay that my college fund is gone. And that all dreams of college and career are dead. At least things are better between me and mom. Almost losing her has made me appreciate her more.

Mom's different, too. She's quiet, tentative, almost embarrassed. "I could have hurt people," she says. "Or destroyed their homes. I couldn't have lived with that."

She starts setting her alarm clock every morning, getting up without my help.

"I thought you couldn't get up to an alarm clock," I say.

"Sure I can!" She gives me an indignant look.

"Would you show me how you keep track of orders on the computer?" she asks. "Your system seems to work really well."

I spend an evening teaching her, and she gets the hang of it pretty quickly.

"I can't believe the Broadmans gave you all that money," she says.

Now it's coming.

"It was really wonderful of you to contribute your only money to fixing the house. Thank you, sweetie."

Lester calls right after the fire and gets the whole story. Then he doesn't call for five days, which is a long time for him. He had warned Mom he was going on a retreat where no cell phones were allowed, but we've heard stories like that before. Mom walks around with the most terrible sad, drawn look on her face. She's used to being abandoned. For that matter, so am I.

• • •

I call Roy to thank him for donating and to talk about the research project.

"The fire took me off it for a while," I tell him. "But I'm back on now."

"Have you worked out how much data you'll need to collect over what period of time?" Roy asks. "And where you're going to store all the data samples you collect, and how you'll go about testing them?"

I have to think it all through and spell out each step in my research plan. "Okay. I'll get back to you soon," I promise.

"But Alex? It looks really good so far."

"Thanks." Deep down, I know he's right. I have a lot of work to do, but I can already see it's going to be awesome.

• • •

I continue to meet Jeremy every night to hang out at Dizzy's or on the Sea Walk. Since Disneyland, we're better friends than ever, although sometimes he has this look of longing on his face, like a little boy who wants a puppy he can't have. I'm just glad for his friendship and almost never think about our kiss in the hot tub and what might have happened if things had been different with him and Jennifer.

Taking a course through Nate's Dive Shop, he has gotten his Open Water Certification. He tells me that now he wants to dive some of the more remote spots on the island. "And you're gonna be my partner!"

I'm sitting at the bar at Dizzy's, while Jeremy, who's working, takes a ten minute break. Old tunes from the fifties and sixties crackle through Dizzy's ancient speakers.

"I've already called Kap," Jeremy says, leaning against the bar next to me. "I've booked us for tomorrow."

The words of a song drift by me, *just take a walk to lonely street....* I don't know if Mom's new attitude allows for diving, but I would love to go out on the Sea Princess. The Princess is forty-six feet long, and she's fast and has covered areas out of the sun and storage to keep cameras dry. She carries food and water, a head, and—most beautiful of all to me—rinse hoses and a shower with fresh hot water.

The captain of the Princess, Enrique Silva, has thirty years of experience, and his dive master, Sal Romano, is a pro. Zack's lucky to be working as a deck hand under them.

"When I called for the reservation," Jeremy says, "two couples had already booked the boat for the day, but were open to bringing in a third couple—us—to share the cost with them."

My mind's working. Tomorrow's a cake layer baking day, with no weddings to do. I can stay up late tonight and tomorrow night to get the layers done. Nothing will fall through the cracks.

"How much would it cost?"

"Nothing."

"Jeremy! I feel like a leech. But everything you want to do is so expensive."

"Yeah, well, I'm rich, baby," he says with a swagger. "Take advantage of it." He leans against the bar, surveying his kingdom. Dizzy's is the perfect environment for someone with a Master of Ceremonies temperament, like Jeremy. Today, his Dizzy button says: "I'm not fat. I'm pregnant with ice cream's baby."

"It's in honor of the five pounds I've gained since I got here," he tells me. Selecting his buttons for each work shift is an almost mystical process for him, requiring careful consideration.

"My break's over," he says. "No arguments from you, Missy. You're going with me."

"Where would we go?" I always seem to be asking him that question.

"We're gonna try for Mermaid Harbor." Diving depends so much on the weather and wind conditions at any moment that you can never predict exactly where you'll dive in advance of doing it.

I haven't dived Mermaid Harbor in a long time. And Zack'll be there. I can't resist. "I'll do it," I say. "But I have to talk to Mom about it first."

• • •

I don't fight with Mom or try to hide the truth from her. We're sitting out on our back patio, drinking iced tea. "Diving's just something I have to do. I'm sorry it scares you. I'll be really, really careful."

She listens to me, which is a first. "You don't have any equipment." Her voice roughens, and she drops her eyes, as if she's ashamed.

"Mrs. Broadman sent me all of theirs. I haven't used it, but I've been storing it at Jenna and Dizzy's." I want to put everything out in the open and start over with her, no matter how hard it is.

Mom sits perfectly still, and for a second I think she's going to flare up. Instead, she gets control of herself. "I see," she says in an even voice. "I know you love diving. I'm going to have to get used to it, I guess. But," she wraps both hands around the cold glass of tea. "I just have this bad feeling about you going diving tomorrow."

"After a kelp rescue and a fire, what more could happen to us?" I ask. "You know what they say: lightning never strikes twice in the same place."

"Lightning *did* strike twice," she points out. "And they also say that trouble comes in threes."

"I'll be really careful," I promise. I've never been superstitious.

"We're on," I tell Jeremy.

Chapter Twenty-Two

The next morning I meet Jeremy at seven forty five on the pier in Paradise Harbor. The Sea Princess waits for us there, white and pristine, with a row of air tanks neatly lined up in their rack. After a raid on Jenna and Dizzy's garage, our dive bags bulge with Broadman equipment, all much slicker and high-end than anything I've ever owned before.

Glancing around, I see no sign of Zack. *Stop it,* I order my heart, as it begins to pound. I show Jeremy the bin for his gear and put his camera in a water-tight storage cupboard. He always seems to spread himself and his belongings over a large area, which is okay at a fancy resort, but not on a crowded dive boat.

Still no Zack anywhere. I try not to be too obvious in looking for him. "Jeremy, this is Enrique, our captain, and Sal, the dive master."

Enrique sports a salt-and-pepper ponytail, multiple piercings, and tattoos on almost all visible skin. He knows the coastline and dive spots of Santa Rita probably better than any person on earth. Sal, a stocky guy with sad eyes, a kind heart, and four marriages behind him, comes in a close second.

"Hey, Alex," Sal asks, "did you and Zack go looking for The Hulk this year?" The giant fish—a black sea bass—is six feet long and must weigh four hundred pounds. Every year in June, he makes his appearance in Santa Rita waters.

"No. Who saw him first?" For the last three years, Zack and I were the first divers to spot him, winning us an annual ham from Henderson's Groceries.

"Some newbie divers from Rancho Cucamonga," Sal says. "I was taking them down when the fish appears out of nowhere. I didn't think these people would ever notice him. I practically had to bring him over and introduce him."

I feel nostalgic. "Did they win a ham?"

"They did."

"Where *is* Zack Attack?" Enrique asks, stating the question that's on my mind. "It's eight twenty-five already. It's not like him to be late."

"It's not him," Sal says, looking across the harbor into town. "It's the other passengers. I sent Zack over to the Beachcomber to look for them." A moment later, Zack arrives with the rest of our group in tow. These people have made us an hour late leaving, a major breach in diving etiquette.

Zack wears an irritated frown, which mellows into an almost-smile when he sees me, then blackens when he notices Jeremy. He introduces the new passengers.

Standing closest to me is Tom, a thirtyish red-faced guy with one of those voices you can hear from fifty yards away.

"Broadman?" he says when Jeremy's introduced. "Any relation to Broadman Enterprises?"

"I wish," Jeremy replies, a smile creeping onto his face.

"Hey, too bad, huh? I heard they own half of Orange County." Tom honks out a loud laugh.

"I heard they own *all* of Orange County," Jeremy drawls, winking at me with the eye that Tom can't see.

Tom rubs his hands together. "*Wow!* Be nice to get in on a piece o' *that* action, huh?"

"No kidding!" Jeremy gives him a pleasant nod and steers me away.

Zack crouches to put away the two women's heavy equipment in low bins. They both wear short terry-cloth bathing suit cover-ups and rhinestone flip-flops, along with tans that could only come from the Tan Factory. As he finishes with their gear, he stands up, towering over the two women. His eyes seem an even deeper green, and his teeth flash white against his face. "Can I get either of you something to drink?"

The set of his shoulders, the way he surveys the boat, his attentiveness to the passengers—everything about Zack shows that he's found his place: he's just where he wants to be, doing exactly what he wants to do.

My throat constricts, feeling tight and scratchy, as I push aside the fear that I'll never have the chance to feel that way myself.

Zack's dressed for work in a pair of camouflage-patterned swim shorts. As he turns away from the two women, I find myself staring at his muscled back and narrow waist. Jeremy snaps his fingers in front of my eyes, and I jump, my face on fire.

A minute later, Zack passes by with the women's drinks. "Hey Alex." He uses the polite tone of an acquaintance.

"Hey, Zack." The Princess's motor thrums as Enrique maneuvers her though Paradise Harbor. As thrilled as I am to be on the water again, it hurts to see Zack pretending he barely knows me. *I'm* not the one who kissed him and then ran off with someone else.

I sit on a bench under a canopy in the shade, while Jeremy flops down next to me.

"You know, he's hot for you," Jeremy says in my ear.

"Who?"

"Your friend. Aquaman." Jeremy nods toward Zack, who's now talking with Tom and the other guy on board. The Princess bucks as she goes through some chop. While the landlubbers grab for ropes and railings and fall onto benches, Zack barely appears to notice, keeping his balance easily as the boat pitches. He glances over at me as he walks by to get drinks for the two men.

I play innocent. "What are you talking about?"

"I mean that guy Zack cannot keep his eyes off of you. He wants to jump your bones. I can tell."

"No way!" Then a moment later, "Really? You think so?" The idea gives me little thrill of excitement.

"Yeah, I do." Jeremy gets an evil expression on his face. "Let's make him jealous." He slides his arm along the back of my chair and around my shoulders.

I laugh. "You're so bad."

"I know. Act like you love me." He smirks, wiggling his eyebrows.

As I sit there with Jeremy's arm around me, laughing at his silliness, Zack walks up to us, shooting a ferocious look toward Jeremy.

"Can I get either of you something to drink?" His voice sounds choked.

"No!" I yelp out the word, horrified at the thought of Zack waiting on me.

"We're really good right now," Jeremy murmurs, looking at me cow-eyed and nuzzling my hair. His eyes smoldering, Zack stalks away.

The minute Zack's back is turned I slap playfully at Jeremy. "Stop it!" Although I'm giggling, I keep my voice low.

"It's working!" Jeremy whispers. "Look at him!"

Zack's adjusting the air tanks in their rack, pushing and pulling them around with a lot more force than is necessary, especially since the tanks didn't need adjusting to begin with. I start to feel sorry for him, then remember Rosie, naked underneath his tank top, looking out of his bedroom door. My pity evaporates.

The Princess is really making time now, slicing through the water as she heads for Mermaid Harbor. It's about a ninety minute ride from Paradise. We'll dive for an hour, if we can, eat lunch, then return home.

We're in full summer now, late July, and the sun's bright and hot overhead. We're entering Mermaid Harbor. "Look!" I say to

Jeremy, pointing at some black birds floating on the ocean's surface. "Those are cormorants. See them diving?"

Jeremy nods. Every minute or so, a bird up-ends itself and disappears under the water.

"They're eating. That means there are lots of fish and things down there for us to see."

Tom and the other guy are the first divers to leave the boat, disappearing into the water almost as soon as we anchor. Jeremy has a new underwater camera and decides this is the time to do a last minute review of the owner's manual.

"Five minutes!" I tell him. "Then we've gotta go."

Zack helps the two women out on the swim step. One at a time, they disappear into the water.

It seems like it takes us forever to get our gear on. I keep looking out at the water and imagining the sea life waiting for us down there. Mermaid Harbor's an amazing dive site, an underwater mountain whose top ends thirty feet below the surface of the water. Jeremy and I will swim across part of the mountain top first, then dive deeper to explore the sides of the mountain.

"You ready?" I say to Jeremy. We head for the stern, carrying our fins.

Jeremy and I stand on the swim step, Zack beside us. "The two guys," Zack says, "have already been out a long time. You may see them coming up during the beginning of your dive."

"Now no matter what happens," I tell Jeremy, "we stay together." We each take a giant stride into the water and descend. Surrounded by the cool blue-green water, I'm home again, at peace.

I look around, getting my bearings. The sound of my own breathing and the bubbles rising in columns fills my ears. Jeremy's eyes, through his mask, are wide with excitement, which I share.

On the mountain top, the water's full of brilliantly colored fish—tiny blue-banded gobies and senoritas in orange, yellow, or green. Then an enormous school of blacksmith floats by, so vast that the water turns dark around us. Jeremy points to it, goggle-eyed. We float there, unmoving, until, like a thundercloud, it passes and sunlight once again filters through the water.

I love this island. The thought comes suddenly, surprising me. My mother did that much right, by raising me here. I love it, yet I need to leave, go to college, study the oceans and become a scientist.

We come to the edge of the mountain top and look down together. I've told Jeremy about the beautiful bright yellow Zoanthid anemones and the stands of red and golden gorgonian coral fans found in deeper water, down on the side of the underwater mountain. We're at a depth of thirty feet and have agreed to go down as far as fifty. Jeremy nods to me, and we descend again.

As we reach the area thick with anemones, Jeremy hovers a few feet away, with his back to me, taking photographs with his underwater camera. I feel something touch me and turn to find Tom, the loud guy from the boat, whose dive should be ending about now. His eyes are glazed, staring blindly. He slices his hand across his throat. *Out of air.*

Underwater panic. Every diver fears it. It kills divers, and most of all, the inexperienced ones.

My hand goes to my alternative air source, my second regulator. All Tom has to do is take it. He can share my tank with me. But Tom's out of control. He claws at my face, grabs for the regulator in my mouth. I kick my fins hard, trying to back away from him.

Tom's all over me. Wild-eyed, he yanks the regulator from my mouth. I reach for my second regulator, this time for my own use. He must think I'm fighting him—he crushes both arms around me, pinning mine to my body. I almost twist from his grasp, but without air I feel weak and useless.

My alternate air source is right there, inches from my mouth. If I could get it in my mouth, I could breathe. *Think.* Don't panic. Desperate, I crane my neck. Where the hell's Jeremy?

Within seconds, I need to breathe. But my hands are trapped. Even with my air, Tom still listens to his own demons. The regulator, with its precious air, is so close. I *need* to breathe.

Tom's arms clamp around me like a vise, my back toward him. His chest moves in and out against me as he breathes my air in and out. I'm light-headed, black circles dancing in front of me.

A horrible pressure builds inside me, as rage mounts. I want him *off me. Now.*

I curl forward then arch back as hard and fast as I can. The back of my head hits his teeth, while my tank rams him in the chest. He yells, his arms loosening around me.

I grab my air source. Relief makes me giddy. But Tom grabs my arm. The air source drops from my hand. Despair, bitter and full of rage.

I can't think anymore. I'm dizzy. The black circles are huge now and whirl before me.

No air. Swim away. Can't. Where's Jeremy?

I'm dying. Mom.

All the things I never did.

A hand. Something hard on my lips. In my mouth.

I breathe. Sweet, beautiful air.

I breathe again and again. I gasp air into my lungs, filling and refilling them.

Jeremy's here, pushing Tom off me. But Tom's like a wild animal. He heads downward. Since he shares my tank, and I share Jeremy's, he pulls us along with him.

As I breathe deeply, my mind clears. Strength returns to my arms and legs. Jeremy looks at me. The question is in his eyes: what do we do now? Tom still pulls us downward.

All the setbacks and disappointments I've ever had rush over me and crystallize in front of me in the form of this crazy guy. He's going to kill all three of us. That is, unless I stop him.

From deep inside I feel a rush of something—strength, God, adrenaline—probably the same thing that mothers feel in those believe-it-or-not stories when they lift trucks off their toddlers. I am determined. And angry. Angrier than I've ever been in my life.

There's simply no way I'm going to die on account of this fool.

I kick hard with my lower legs and twist suddenly, aiming up toward the surface. Tom is caught by surprise, and he's a weak swimmer to boot. Powering myself forward with my fins and pushing hard with my arms, I turn him around. Jeremy joins me and together the two of us move Tom upward.

We ascend a part of the way, but when we have to make our three minute safety stop, Tom begins to struggle again. In a cold rage, I put both thumbs to his throat and dig in, hard, immobilizing him. Jeremy and I take him the rest of the way up.

As our heads break the water, a yell of relief goes up from the stern of the Sea Princess, where Tom's three friends, along with Enrique, Sal, and Zack have been waiting, scanning for signs of us.

Even as he climbs up the ladder, Jeremy reports to the group. "Tom panicked and took away Alex's air."

Zack pulls me out of the water and lays me on the swim step, where I curl up on my side, suddenly exhausted and unable to move. He crouches next to me, taking off my weight belt, tank, and BCD. I hear his voice in my ear. "God, Alex, are you okay?" I can almost feel his anguish. He helps me up into the boat.

Beside us, Tom's friends have brought him up and helped him with his equipment. He slowly straightens, coughing and shaking his head.

Zack turns to Tom and, in a single motion, drives his fist straight into his jaw, sending him sprawling. Zack falls on him, punching him in the ribs, while Sal and Enrique scramble to pull him off of their paying passenger. I catch the amazement on their faces.

I hear Enrique, sounding small and far away, chewing Zack out. "Man, what's wrong with you? Are you *crazy?*"

"*He's an idiot!*" Zack spits the words. "Alex could have died."

I'm swaying on my feet, and it's not from the motion of the boat. Zack's eyes are so worried, so full of caring and concern, that I can't look at them. I can't be disappointed again. His arms are around me, but as Jeremy walks up, Zack pulls away from me, looking self-conscious.

He sticks his hand out to Jeremy. "Way to go, man," he says. "You saved her life."

"I gave her air, but she got us up. You should've seen her," Jeremy says, shaking the salt water out of his hair. "The warrior mermaid in action!" His glance, full of admiration, hits me like a laser beam of blue light.

I stand there, listening, as if from a great distance, while Jeremy tells them the full story.

"Now wait a minute!" Tom, an ice pack on his face, tries to bluster his way into the conversation with his own side of things.

Jeremy holds up a hand. "Don't even start, dude."

My throat's raw. My head aches, and there's a roaring in my ears. Dimly, I see Zack stealing glances at me, looking concerned. *Don't lead me on, Zack. I know you like Rosie better.* Zack's getting smaller and smaller. The roaring in my ears is getting louder and louder. I shake my head a little, trying to clear it of the confusion I feel.

The boat's tipping to one side. It's going to capsize. I reach out a hand as it pitches wildly.

Zack catches me as I fall.

Chapter Twenty-Three

I lie on the deck in the bow of the Sea Princess, Zack kneeling next to me. Groggy, I blink my eyes against the light. "What happened?"

Zack helps me up to a sitting position. "You fainted. The others are in the stern."

I groan, holding my head. "Why would I faint?"

"Maybe shock. But… you probably want me to get Jeremy for you." He says it as half a statement, half a question.

I shake my head. "No. It's okay."

Zack smiles, then says in an offhand way, "You wanna rinse off?" He knows the first thing I do after diving is to strip off my wet suit and shower away the salt water—particularly with hot, fresh water if I can get it.

"Yes." My voice sounds very small, even to me.

I quiver inside as he helps me stand and unzips the front of my wet suit. He pulls it gently off my arms and then down my legs, crouching to pull my feet out, while my insides melt into hot fudge. Given the danger that I could fall and hurt myself, I'm forced to lean on him for support. As hazy and disoriented as I am, I somehow manage to remember that I'm wearing my new and really cute red bikini today. From the expression on his face, I can tell Zack has noticed.

"Here." Zack pulls a rinse hose toward us and starts the water. Nice boats like the Princess carry fresh water for showering in tanks that absorb heat from either the sun or the boat's engine.

Total, blissful heaven. Zack sprays the warm water on my shoulders and back, then through my hair. It feels delicious on my cold, shivery skin. He's getting wet, too, but he doesn't seem to mind. I'm feeling better but, just to be on the safe side, I continue to lean against his bare chest. Zack doesn't seem to mind that either.

Jeremy drifts into my thoughts again, then right back out. He'll be fine for a little while, hanging with the crew and passengers

Zack rinses me off with one hand, holding me close to him with the other. The warm water runs down my back and legs. I close my eyes and drift, pressed up against him. Then he wraps us up in a couple of big towels, and we lie down in the sun.

I lie with my head on his chest, listening to the beating of his heart, flooded with emotion—joy, relief, lust, and nerves. I push out a deep sigh.

"Alex?" he says in a quiet voice. "What happened to us? That day on the mountain?" His forehead creases, and he runs his hand through his hair.

I try to remember, distracted by the feeling of his chest under my hand. I'm so happy right now I feel like I'm floating six inches above the deck. "You were talking about dating. And all I could think of was Mom. I didn't want to be like Mom."

He inhales sharply. "You were thinking about your *mother?*"

"Well, yeah. I mean, about how every time Mom dates a guy, it's a disaster. I was afraid of doing the same thing."

"Oh. I thought you didn't like me enough to… to.."

"I did. Like you, I mean. But I wasn't expecting… I didn't know what to say."

"Hey, you two." It's Sal, scratching his head and looking at the deck, out to sea, at anything except at us. "How you doing, Alex?"

Not now! I'm not ready to end this conversation. "Fine! Thanks, Sal." I untangle myself from my towel, pulsing with disappointment.

"Zack, we're coming in."

Zack's eyes meet mine and in them is a promise of more. We smile at each other. He springs to his feet.

I find Jeremy in the captain's quarters yakking with Enrique and learning how to guide the boat. "Next time, Alex, I'm driving this thing!" he says, but immediately leaves Enrique to join me.

"You okay?" he asks me, giving my shoulders a squeeze.

I nod my head. I'm better than okay.

As the Sea Princess arrives at the pier in Paradise Harbor, Jeremy and I gather up our bags, ready to go. Zack's working, lashing the Princess to the pier and putting down a gangplank. I wave to him, feeling suddenly shy, and he waves back, stopping his work to watch me leave the boat.

Tom and his companions sit quietly in the bow with their bags. I realize that the other three know only what Tom has told them, and I'm not sure what Tom even remembers.

As we pass by them, Tom looks down and away, unwilling to meet my eyes. I keep going. I'm alive. That's all that matters.

Chapter Twenty-Four

Mom's on the phone in the kitchen. She leans her weight against the counter while she runs one bare toe along the chipped vinyl flooring. Even with my new policy of full disclosure, I haven't dared tell her what happened to me in Mermaid Harbor.

She has painted her toenails apricot and looks very young in a halter-top and shorts. Because we're going to bake, she and I have both pulled our hair into tight ponytails, mine long and hers a little tuft that sticks out in back. "Great ... okay," she's saying, punctuating her speech with spurts of laughter. She smiles, with her head cocked to one side, while I pull baking pans out of a cupboard. By the time she's off the phone, I'll have everything in place and ready to go.

"That was Lester," she says, hanging up. Her cheeks are pink and her eyes bright with excitement.

I look at her in surprise. We haven't heard from him for a week. "Alex, he wants me to come with him to his twenty-fifth year college reunion." She clasps her hands together in front of her. "He says he wants to show me off!"

If he can deal with Mom's tendency to set things on fire, Lester's made of tougher stuff than I thought. "That's great, Mom! Where's the reunion?" I place a set of mixing bowls on the counter and pull out the measuring spoons.

"In Burbank. I'd go on Saturday morning and return Sunday afternoon."

I stop moving. "We have five cakes this weekend."

She waves her hand in the air. "You can handle them, Alex."

Needless to say, she would never—could never—do this for me. "I guess." My voice sounds the way I suddenly feel, rebellious and grudging.

For the first time since the fire, she gets that petulant look on her face. "I deserve this! I never go anywhere!"

She never goes anywhere. The unfairness of it's like a slap. I remind myself that I want this thing with Lester to work out. With a sigh, I open my laptop and study the weekend schedule. The cakes are all standard designs that I can do myself, and two of the weddings are in the evening, which gives me more time to make the deliveries. "I think I could manage this weekend on my own."

She claps her hands. "You see, Alex? There's always a way!"

"*But.*"

She stops clapping.

"You owe me one." I glower at her. "The next time I need something, you have to return the favor."

"Well, of course," she says, surprised and indignant.

"Good." I plan to hold her to it.

She tells Lester she'll go.

• • •

"Kap chewed me out royally," Zack says, "for jumping that dude who almost killed you." He has waited four days after the dive trip to call me.

"I'm sorry. Thanks for standing up for me." I flop back on my bed, my cell phone to my ear.

"It was worth it." A silence falls. "Do you want to go mountain biking? Monday's my day off."

154

I hesitate. I can justify taking Monday off, since I'll be working all weekend while Mom's with Lester. But there's another problem. "What about Rosie?"

Zack's voice is earnest. "I've been thinking a lot. I'm seeing her Friday. I'm gonna tell her I want to take a break."

"A *break*? You mean, like, a break-up?"

"I guess." His voice turns flat and bleak.

I don't blame him for dreading that conversation. "Okay, Monday then." I can hardly believe it. I've got a date with Zack.

• • •

I have the weekend so well organized that my five deliveries fly by without a hitch. When my mom comes back Sunday afternoon, all the cakes have reached their destinations, the customers are happy, and I'm lying on my bed reading.

She bursts into my room, practically lighting it up with her excitement. "Oh, Alex, I had such a good time! Lester introduced me to all his old friends. He said he was *proud* to have me by his side. Those were his exact words!" She looks younger and prettier than she's been in a long time.

It gives me a good feeling to see my mom so happy. "Of course he'd be proud! He sounds like a smart guy."

"Thanks, sweetie." She plumps down in my old beanbag chair and tells me all about it. We open a bottle of sparkling cider and call for Chinese food, which we put on trays and eat outside on the back patio. The night air is soft and balmy, and the fronds of palm trees rustle in the breeze.

"Full moon," I say, tipping my head skyward.

"We better lock our doors tonight! And look—fortune cookies!" Mom tosses me one, and we tear simultaneously at the cellophane wrappers.

"Me first!" Mom takes one end of her fortune in each hand and reads, "*A secret admirer will soon send you a sign of affection.* That's a good one!" she crows. "Maybe Lester's going to give me a present!"

"It said a *secret* admirer. That means someone else likes you too!"

"Maybe, but I'll bet he's not as good as Lester."

"You really like him?" This is working out beyond my wildest dreams.

"Alex, I think he's the nicest man I've ever met." She sits up very straight in her lawn chair, her hands folded in her lap. "And he likes me and wants to see me all the time!"

"I'm glad." I beam at her, unable to believe her good luck and mine.

Maybe, in her current mood, Mom will be open to a suggestion.

"I've been thinking… we're doing so well with our cakes. What if we raised our prices just a little? It's been fifteen years since the last increase, and our prices are lower than even cakes on the mainland."

A frown settles on Mom's forehead. "Honey, raising prices is bad public relations."

"It doesn't have to be. Mom, our prices are so low, we don't have a chance of making any real money."

"We'll make money by having lots of customers," Mom says.

"A small price increase could make us an extra $20,000 a year—in profit!"

But she's not convinced.

"Promise me you'll think about it."

She nods. It's the best I'll get from her tonight.

After a second, I look at my own fortune.

If you continually give, you will continually have. I read it aloud to Mom, who shrugs.

"You'll get a better one next time," she says.

I think about it. If I continually give, I'll continually have. Have what? More wedding cakes to make?

It's just a fortune cookie. I crumple it and toss it in the trash.

• • •

Zack arrives at my door on his bicycle, a rolled up blanket tied to the back of his seat, and carrying a stuffed backpack. "I brought a picnic," he says.

We set off down Cinnamon Street and take Sapphire Road out of town toward the base of Mount Alejandro. Outside of the tiny area that the town occupies, there are virtually no level surfaces on Santa Rita Island.

Just where the fire road starts is a eucalyptus grove, heavily shaded and fragrant from the tall trees. People have taken to leaving bowls of food for the many wild cats on the island. It isn't a good idea, as it increases the numbers of wild and sometimes rabid cats that prowl around Santa Rita, yowling at night and getting into fights. But we all do it anyway. Zack has brought a zip lock bag full of kibble, which we dump in one of the bowls.

We take the fire road up the mountain, winding our way straight up for a continuous three miles. It calls for thigh and calf muscles of steel, along with a titanium heart, but Zack and I are used to it. Ignoring the burning in my legs and lungs, I match Zack movement for movement. We settle into a steady rhythm, looking out at the ocean and down into canyons as we pedal along.

Finally, we arrive at the summit, where a look-out offers a 360-degree view. Zack and I stand there for a while, trying to identify and name different diving sites along the coast down below. "Someday when I have my own boat, I'll take people out to all those places," Zack says, "Maybe do two- and three-day excursions."

"How do you know for sure that's what you want to do?" I ask. My exact dream job is still out there, waiting for me to come and find it.

"I dunno. I just always have." He slips an arm around my waist.

"What happened with Rosie?" I lean my head on his shoulder, thinking, I've waited a long time to do that.

He slumps. "It was bad. She cried."

I don't say anything. Maybe I really am a selfish person. All this time I was longing for Zack, I never thought about Rosie for a minute, at least, not about her feelings. It sounds like she got hurt. He catches my look. "I really did it this time," he promises, looking far off across the water to the mainland. A muscle tightens in his jaw. When he turns to me again a minute later, his face is unreadable. "Let's eat," he says.

Zack leads me over to a grassy spot in the shade of some trees, with a view of the ocean. He spreads out his blanket on the grass and starts pulling things out of his backpack.

I have to smile, seeing the food. Here are all my favorites: Heavenly Deviled Eggs, peanut butter and jelly sandwich fingers, carrot curls, fruit salad, and Chunky Chocolate Chip cookies. We stuff ourselves and then lie on the blanket.

"I guess I'll have to thank Jenna for this lunch."

"Hey, I carried it up the mountain for you." Zack gives me one of his heartstopping smiles, reaches out a hand, and tickles me in the ribs. He knows how I'll react.

I scream and writhe away from him, grabbing his hands. "Don't you dare!"

"Sorry. That was an accident." Zack gives me a fiendish grin and attacks me from another angle, tickling my waist and side. I shriek and wiggle on the blanket, all the while making plans for a counter attack. Knowing his feet are sensitive, I dive for them, grabbing one and running my fingers along its bare sole.

He yelps, then comes after me, using one hand to hold both of my wrists over my head, while he pulls me toward the ground.

"Omigod, a buffalo!" I yell.

He falls for it, jerking his head around, which gives me the chance to push him backward and throw my leg over him, putting him on his back while I sit on him.

"Gotcha!" I crow. We're both panting and laughing. He still has both my hands in an iron grip.

"Okay, you got me," Zack drawls. "*Now* what're you gonna do with me?"

I stop laughing as he straightens his arms over his head, bringing me down until I'm lying on top of him, our faces an inch apart.

"Alex," he says, and my heart starts a heavy pounding in my chest. And then, finally, after all those weeks that I imagined it, he kisses me. And I kiss him back, going all melty inside and moving as close to him as I can get. He tastes of chocolate and smells of the ocean. I want to devour him.

We roll over onto our sides, facing each other. Zack's body is pressed up against mine. My hands are running down his back. I have never been kissed like this before, with deep, exploring kisses that go on for a long time. I've never had a boy slide his hand up inside my shirt and undo my bra. Never felt a boy touch my breasts. Something inside me jumps and makes me hope he'll keep doing it. Zack's hands are slow and gentle, like he has all day.

Except then he starts to slip my T-shirt up over my head. *Whoa.* I put my hand on his, and he stops.

"Is it okay?" he asks.

"It's just—a little faster than I expected." I look up at him, blushing, feeling silly.

He gives me a wry grin. "What are you waiting for—to get to know me better?" His tone is gentle, ironic, which takes any possible sting out of the comment.

He's right. What *am* I waiting for?

I look around. We're completely alone on the top of this mountain. I'm almost eighteen. I've known Zack all my life. I love him in some way that I can't yet define, whether it's friend love, or passion, or forever love. I definitely lust for him; that I know.

My hand tightens on his. I want to, but something stops me. "I can't go this fast. I'm not ready." I hear the regret in my voice.

Zack's head drops for a second. "All right," he says, but his tone says it isn't. I've already learned that Zack doesn't deal well with rejection. I hesitate a moment. Longing wells up inside of me. *Do it.*

But, again, something stops me. I need more time, or maybe something else. Not sure of what it is, the only thing I can do is put the brakes on. I'm going to wait until I'm ready.

• • •

We start seeing each other almost every evening, if only for an hour or two—and now we're not diving. Our fins and tanks sit neglected as we spend whatever time we have tangled together on an air mattress in the back of Zack's pick up. He knows every remote spot on the island, it seems, and nothing thrills me more than to lie there with him, in the cool evening air, looking—or not looking—at the stars.

Being with Zack in his truck is fun and sexy, and it makes me feel like a bad girl. Although, the truth is, I don't want to be that bad, at least not right away.

"I need to take this slowly," I tell Zack, even as his fingers play with the waistband of my shorts.

"How slowly?" he teases me, as his hands move lower.

"I'm not ready to have sex."

"It's okay," he says, although I know he'd like to.

He's used to getting a lot more from Rosie, who is not taking the break-up well. I find out they've been talking when Zack takes a call from her around eleven o'clock at night, as we lie together in the back of his truck. He glances at the display, gets a worried look on his face, and says to me, "This'll just take a sec."

"Hey," he answers the phone, sounding as if he gets calls from her all the time. I'm outraged to see him smiling. "I only have a minute, okay?" He listens. "Because I'm with Alex." He listens some more. "Not right now." Rosie's talking again. "Okay, look, I gotta go. I'll talk to you about it tomorrow, okay?"

Tomorrow? We lie on our sides, facing each other, Zack's leg draped over both of mine. I kick his leg off of me and sit up. "What do you mean tomorrow? You're going to call her back?"

"Just to talk about our break-up. She says we need to…," he searches for the words, "…process our feelings." Process his feelings? Zack hasn't processed a feeling in his entire life, or if he did, it gave him heartburn.

"What kind of BS is Rosie feeding you?"

Zack flounders. "She's having a hard time. She needs to talk to me." When I gape at him, he adds, "Don't worry. It's just for closure."

"Closure?" The Zack I grew up with thinks that zippers are for closure.

"So how much have you been talking to Rosie? For… closure?" He swallows hard. "I dunno. Once or twice."

"Well, okay, then." That's not so bad. "If you've only talked once or twice since you broke up…"

Zack swallows even harder. "Once or twice. A day."

A day? "I think you need to put some closure to these conversations!" I glower at him as I crawl around on the mattress, buttoning my shirt and looking for my shoes.

Zack groans. "Aw, come on, Alex. It's over with me and Rosie."

"You talk to her every day on the phone, and you say it's over!" I've missed two buttons on my shirt, so it's hanging crooked. I start to fix it, but I'm too upset to bother with it.

"Look, she's still my friend!" Zack grabs my hand. "When I was dating her, she didn't say I had to drop *you!*"

I stop looking for my shoes. I sit down on the mattress. "This is different," I say—weakly, because I'm not exactly sure how it's different. I search my memory for what I know about his relationship with Rosie. How long did they go out? Five months, I think.

"So, what was the deal with you and Rosie?" I ask, finally. "Did you really like her?"

"Yeah." He sets his jaw defiantly. "I did really like her."

"Were you guys serious?" I can hardly believe it. As much as we like each other, neither Zack nor I are ready for commitment and long-term relationships. We have too many other things we want to do first, things that take us in different directions.

Zack squirms. "She might have been." He looks off into space. "And you?"

He shrugs, not answering my question.

"If you really liked her, why did you decide to start seeing me?"

"Because… I dunno. I guess I've always pictured myself with you. We've always been together."

He makes me sound like a pair of old shoes he can't bear to give away.

"You were having sex with her, right?"

For a minute, I think he's going to deny it. But he can't. I practically caught them in the act. "Yeah." He sighs a little.

"Are you mad at me because I haven't had sex with you yet?"

He squirms some more. "It would be cool if you did. But I'm not mad at you. At least, not super mad," he admits.

I flop onto my back on the air mattress and put my hands behind my head. "Maybe it *is* better just to be friends. Like with Jeremy. He and I have no complications. He has a girlfriend, so he doesn't want to have sex with me."

"Trust me," Zack says. "He wants to have sex with you."

"No, he doesn't. He's faithful to her."

"Doesn't matter. Even if he's faithful to her, he still wants to sleep with you."

I think about it. If Jeremy's attracted to me, he's got a weird way of showing it.

Zack and I talk in circles for a while, agreeing on nothing, until he drives me home. As we pull up to my house, he gives me a shrewd look and says, "I'll make you a deal. I'll give up Rosie's friendship if you give up Jeremy's."

I can't give up Jeremy's friendship. Even as busy as I am with work, seeing Zack in the evenings, and working on my research plan for Roy, I still drop by Dizzy's almost every day for my Jeremy fix and have lunch with him a couple of times a week. Faced with the possibility of losing him, letting Zack talk to Rosie seems like a small price to pay.

• • •

Jeremy's nearing the end of his stay on the island. I've come to think of him as my rock, my most trusted friend. I can't bear the thought of him leaving.

But lately, he's been acting mysterious. A couple of times, when I've called him at the Inn, knowing he was there, I've gotten no answer. When I asked where he's been, he says only "Around" or changes the subject completely. A couple of times, he's been unable to see me, his explanation again being a vague "Just busy, I guess."

"What are you up to?" I ask him finally. "What's the big secret?"

"You'll see. One of these days." And that's all he'll say.

This week, Jeremy hasn't even had time for lunch with me. I've mainly seen him at Dizzy's during his breaks from work. He and Dizzy have gotten really tight. Jeremy has a million questions about the restaurant: how the kitchen's managed, the staff schedules, the ordering of supplies. Sometimes, he helps Dizzy when he's overloaded, scheduling and calling in temporary help as needed.

At Jeremy's suggestion, Dizzy has ordered a load of bumper stickers, which I help put up on the walls one day. The three of us open the box together, spreading the stickers out on a table for inspection.

"A wise man wrote this one," Dizzy says, holding up *Do not play leap frog with a unicorn.* Wincing, I show them one that says *I don't make mistakes; I date them.* "This one's for Mom."

"Not anymore," Jeremy reminds me.

True. Lester's been coming out to the island almost every week, usually for a couple of days mid-week, always taking the same room at the Seashell Hotel. He's got his own company, so he can make his own schedule and bring work out with him, too. He and Mom hold hands and talk to each other in low, intimate voices. They grin like idiots and laugh for no reason. Lester seems to bring out the best in her, making her calmer, kinder, and easier to be around.

"He wants to take us both to lunch," Mom tells me. "When he's out here next. He says he wants to get to know you better—he wants to know all about us!"

163

She's practically humming with happiness.

Not half as much as I am.

• • •

I braid my hair into a rope down my back, put on a simple yellow shift and sandals, and go to meet them at the Buccaneer at noon on Wednesday. Lester, sitting at a table on the outside deck, waves me over to an empty chair across from him, and then volunteers to move his own chair over so we can both sit in the shade of the umbrella.

"Sue's still at the Hand Stand. Her manicure's running late, I'm afraid." He gives me his cheerful gap-toothed grin and hands me a menu. "It hasn't even started. She said to order without her, and she'll join us when she can."

We both order the fish and chips, along with two iced teas, and we talk for a while about Jessica's wedding.

"By the way, I have to thank you," he says, holding out his glass in a toast.

"Why?" I clink my glass with his.

"Jessica told me it was your idea to…" he fidgets for moment, as if embarrassed, "introduce me to your mother. Well done!"

"You're welcome." Maybe there's hope. For me to live my own life someday. I'm pleased, but struggle to think of what to say. "It's a long way for you to come every week, with the boat ride and all."

"It's my pleasure." Our fish and chips arrive. "So much for the old cholesterol count," he says, rolling his eyes at me as if to imply, *But hey, when you're a wild and crazy guy, you just gotta go for it.*

He's a nerd, all right. But a sweet one.

Uneasiness trickles through me. I've always assumed Lester could handle my mother and take care of himself in this relationship. What if I'm wrong?

"Thanks for holding down the fort while Sue came to my reunion." He dips a fry in ketchup.

"It was no problem. Now I know I can deliver five cakes in two days all on my own."

His fork stops halfway to his mouth. "Five cakes?"

"Yeah, that's normal for a weekend. In the summer."

Lester looks at me with curiosity. "How do you even do that?"

So Mom doesn't talk to him much about her business. I'm not surprised. I shouldn't be talking to him now myself, but my jaw seems to have come unhinged. It's flapping up and down, completely out of control.

"You have to be really organized. You have to make all the layers in advance, schedule the cakes with enough time in between them, make sure the van's packed with all the supplies. Stuff like that."

Lester's eyebrows tie themselves into a knot on his forehead. "I didn't realize my reunion was so much work for you."

I wave my hand airily. "It wasn't that different from usual. Except Mom normally decorates some of the weekend cakes and bakes some layers." I don't know what's making me blab to Lester like this. Maybe I want him to know that she needs help. That I need help.

Or maybe I'm trying to help him.

Lester sets his fork and knife carefully across his plate. He has the stern look of a high school prinicipal about to lay out the discipline.

Uh-oh. Maybe I said too much.

"How many hours a week do you work for your mom?"

"In the summer, it amounts to a full-time job. Winter's a lot lighter."

"I would hope so. You're in school then!" Lester's eyes widen in alarm. "At least you have a lot of spending money!" He looks over at me for confirmation, then realizes he won't be getting any. His mouth sets in a thin line, as if a bad smell has just wafted into the room.

"Tell me a little more about yourself," he says, as a seagull lands on the railing not far from him, squawks, and flaps away.

"There's not a lot to tell," I say, then once again find myself spewing, now about my school work and my hopes for the future. A part of me knows I should shut my mouth, but it feels so good to unburden myself that I just keep going.

"I wanted to study oceanography this summer— it didn't work out. But I have this really cool research project planned for my senior year. I'll be diving and gathering data, and it's going to be really interesting."

"Where would you like to go to college?"

"I'm not sure. Something close by, probably." I manage to shut up and not say anything more.

"You're quite an impressive young lady." Lester blinks rapidly, which I've noticed he does when he gets agitated. He rolls a straw wrapper between his fingers, demolishing it.

I can't believe I've done this. I've said way more than Mom would have wanted me to. But Lester had to know.

Lester answers a ring from his cell, than hangs up. "Sue's not going to make it. We'll pick her up at the Hand Stand after we're done." He fishes a roll from the bread basket and butters it.

"Do you mind if I ask you, Alex, what kind of relationship you have with your mother? That is, if you want to tell me." He stops, as if afraid he's gone too far.

I pick at my napkin, folding and unfolding it. That way, I don't have to look at him. I feel like I owe him the truth. But I want to be fair to my mother, too.

"It's always been just me and her," I say. "My dad left before I was born." In moments of sympathy toward her, I've imagined how hard it must have been for my mother, completely alone, pregnant, and later, with an infant to care for. She was nineteen, only two years older than I am now.

"She's always been fantastic at baking, so she started making wedding cakes for one of the resorts. But she's not good at business. We always struggled, and I grew up helping her. It's all either of us knows." I'm speaking slowly, carefully choosing each word. In a way, I'm telling myself the story as much as I'm telling him.

"She never remarried. We live in such a small place, you know, and she didn't have opportunities to meet people." Am I glossing over the truth here? Mom's dated over the years. But they weren't good men. Or they weren't good to her, anyway.

"So, I guess she came to rely on me more and more. And in way, I didn't mind. It made me feel … important, I guess."

I've never realized that before. Until now, telling Lester. I liked feeling smarter and better than my mother. In a way, I encouraged it.

It seems like a weird way for a kid to feel. But I liked feeling strong and in charge. I liked that she depended on me. It meant she needed me. That she'd never leave me.

Lester's face is expressionless. I wonder what he's thinking. It's strange how I feel this urge to protect Mom, to cover for her. "So, maybe," I say to him, "we fell into some bad habits, you know? And now, she depends on me, and I want to leave for college. So it's hard. But we get along much better since the fire. I think, with some good business advice and a helper, she'd be fine without me."

I sit there thinking, *did I tell Lester the truth?* I decide I have. And I realize that Zack's been right all along. I've played a role in the way that Mom and I have ended up. The needy, dependent person that she's become— I helped create it.

I look over at Lester again to gauge his reaction.

He makes a skeptical face at me. "So it's all your fault?"

"Not my *fault,* exactly…"

"Look, Alex, I understand what you're trying to say. But, bottom line— you were a kid. Sue was the adult in the situation." His voice is final, saying *that's that.*

Wait a minute. I wanted him to like her. I wanted it work out between them.

Lester finishes paying the bill. "Let's go find Sue." His voice is stern, his face set in a grim mask

• • •

167

Mom marches into my bedroom that evening, her face red and blotchy from crying.

Here it comes.

"Lester just raked me over the coals, asking me a million questions. About you!"

I sit up on my bed, looking at her cautiously. *"Me?"* I try not to sound guilty, but I do.

"Yes, you! What did you tell him anyway? He acted like I was some kind of criminal!" She gives me an angry, reproachful look.

"I just told him what I do for the business." I'm dying inside. Why did I have to be such a motor mouth?

But all I did was tell the truth, after all.

"He's really mad at me." Mom's eyes are bright with tears. "He said I work you too hard and don't pay you. That you need to go to college. He said," she stops, her face twisting with fear, "he's not sure what kind of person I am anymore. He's going to think about it, and we'll talk when he comes back out next week."

I try to gather my thoughts. "I'm sorry you're unhappy, Mom. I told Lester the truth. About my life." In a way, I *am* sorry. I wanted this to work between them. But Lester had to find out eventually.

"What truth?" Mom's eyes are wounded. "That you work in the family business? What's wrong with that?" She paces back and forth. "And haven't I been nice?" Her face drops a little. "Lately?"

"You *have* been nicer," I say. "Look, he's coming back out again. So he hasn't given up on you. Talk to him, and listen to what he has to say." I nod encouragingly. "Compromise."

She runs into her bedroom and slams the door.

I stand up slowly from the bed I've been sitting on. I ache all over inside. I want to cry, but my eyes are dry and hot. My dirty clothes from yesterday are scattered on the floor, and a couple of sticky juice glasses stand on my desk. I think about picking them up but I don't. I have the rest of my life to clean up this room.

I look at my watch. It's eight thirty. I'm seeing Zack at ten, after the Princess gets back from a late dive.

I call Jeremy. "Meet me on the Seawalk?"

"Sure."

As usual, seeing Jeremy will make me feel better. But in a couple of weeks, he'll be gone. I feel lonely just thinking about it.

Chapter Twenty-Five

"Can you be here on Tuesday night? Nine o'clock? Or will you be taking a spin in the *Zackmobile?*" Jeremy skewers me with a look.

My face goes hot. We're sitting together at the bar at Dizzy's during Jeremy's lunch hour. Since the blow-up of Mom and Lester's relationship, my insides feel like they've been passed through a blender.

"There's not *that* much going on in the Zackmobile. For your information."

"Yeah, right." Jeremy leans his elbows on the bar, smirking at me.

I move on. "Is this thing on Tuesday the surprise you've been talking about?"

"Yep. And bring anyone you want—Zack, your mom, whoever."

I'll invite Zack, for sure. And Mom too, as a peace offering, although she's barely speaking to me. She drifts around the house in her nightgown, sniffling into tissues and checking her phone for messages from Lester. But he hasn't called.

Part of me thinks I'm a dummy, saying all that stuff to Lester. Now my chance for escape has shrunk down to the size of a grain of sand. But part of me knows I did the right thing.

"While we're on the subject of invitations," Jeremy says, "what are you doing Labor Day weekend?"

"Seven cakes," I groan. Of course, I have to work. Labor Day's one of our huge wedding weekends.

"Can you get the weekend off?"

"No. Why?" Somehow, I don't think Mom's going to be repaying me that favor she owed.

"Gramps is turning seventy, and we're having a party over Labor Day. Just the family and special family friends. You're on the short list."

I catch my breath. "Omigod, I would love to go."

"The party's on Sunday, but Gram and Gramps want you to come a day earlier. The whole family's staying at their house for the weekend. That includes you."

They want me to stay with them!

"Where's their house?"

"Pasadena. Just east of Los Angeles." He leans into me. "C'mon! You gotta keep me company."

I shake my head. "There's no way. It's a crazy weekend for us. One person can't handle it alone." Angry rebellion fills me as I admit to myself how much I want to go.

"Can someone else help your mom?"

I think about it. "I don't see who. Maybe I can brainstorm up an idea." I'll put it on the list as one more knotty problem to be solved.

• • •

On Tuesday evening, I walk over to Dizzy's Dive by myself, feeling down. I asked Zack to come, but his dad needs him for something. I asked Mom, hoping she'd come along, but she refused my invitation, saying she was going to take a sleeping pill and go to bed early.

Jeremy has reserved a table in front of the karaoke stage, where Jenna and I are supposed to sit. She's already there when I arrive. With her is Evelyn Armor, who has obviously taken a rare night off from her management duties up at the Inn.

"Hi, Evelyn," I say, wondering what she's doing here.

Dizzy walks onto the stage and taps the microphone. "Hello, folks." He waits for the unusually large crowd to settle down. "Tonight," he says. "Dizzy's Dive is proud to provide a little live entertainment. So without further ado..." He steps off the stage, and there, carrying guitars and working their way through the crowd from the back office, where they've been hiding, are Jeremy and— Rebecca Armor.

Jeremy grins and waves to the crowd, many of whom he's managed to meet in his weeks on the island. He's in one of his casually expensive white cotton shirts, open at the neck, with khaki pants. But the revelation is Rebecca. In a peasant blouse and long flowered skirt, her hair done up, she looks prettier than I've ever seen her. She's holding tight to the neck of her guitar, while Jeremy shoots her a reassuring smile.

"Evelyn, did you know about this?" I stage-whisper to her.

"They've been practicing for two weeks. But Rebecca wouldn't let us tell anyone." Evelyn shifts in her seat and gives Rebecca a little wave.

Now I understand why the place is so crowded tonight. In addition to the summer folks, there are a lot of locals who usually stay away from Dizzy's during high season. Evelyn and Dizzy must have recruited them.

And with that, Rebecca starts to play. We all know her as Evelyn's oddball daughter. But who knew this girl could *wail* on the guitar? And *sing*. Rebecca's voice is smoky and sweet and raspy all at the same time, and when she gets going, with that voice and her guitar riffs or runs, or whatever they're called, she *rocks*.

Jeremy mainly sings harmony, but he has a strong, clear voice. Some of the songs I recognize, but most of them, it turns out, Rebecca has written.

I should be happy for her, but it *kills* me to see Rebecca in her element, doing the thing she was clearly put on earth to do. I clap and cheer with the rest of the crowd, trying to ignore the jealousy that has rooted in me and is growing—fast.

Get over it, I command myself.

And then there's Jeremy. Why didn't he tell me about this? I thought he and I were close—special friends, even. Clearly I've been wrong.

I sit there feeling completely alone in the world. In my mind I see Zack's eyes, his arms and chest, feel him pull me close to him, and long for him to be here with me. I remember the last time I saw him and how much I wanted him. But I kept telling him no. At the moment, I can't imagine why.

Jeremy and Rebecca do six songs, plus two encores, and finally make their escape. One small, decent part of me is glad to see the happiness on Rebecca's face, even as I grind my teeth, absurdly jealous of her and her talent and all the time she's gotten to spend with Jeremy. Don't be such a baby. It's no big deal.

Afterward, I fight my way through the crowd around Rebecca. "You were incredible!" I'm just able to say it, before she's swept off by a throng of admirers. Then, Jeremy's standing beside me. "You were wonderful!" I say to him. "When did all this start?"

"A few weeks ago," he says, looking sideways at me. "I heard her singing and playing and then we started singing together."

"Well, you were great!" I say, thinking again of Zack. What am I looking for anyway? When will anything ever happen for me? There's no exciting future waiting for me in some romantic, faraway setting.

Jeremy, Evelyn, and Rebecca climb into a golf cart to return to the Inn. I wave good-bye and stand there as they drive away.

Something special happened tonight for Rebecca. I need something special, too. I have all this hunger and need inside of me, and it has nowhere to go. Maybe tonight's the night for me and Zack.

In that moment, I decide. I'll give Zack another call, see if he's done helping his dad. He'll come to me and, this time, I'll be ready.

Clouds scud across the dark sky, while the moon plays peek-a-boo behind them. A small, rubber Zodiak trolls its way through the moored boats, returning a family from the shore to its floating home. I love Paradise Harbor at night.

A couple strolls along the Seawalk, deep in conversation, and my glance passes over the two, then returns to rest on them. It's dark, and I squint at them as I punch in the number to speed dial Zack. In my ear, I hear the ringing of his phone, matched by a familiar ring tone out on the Seawalk. I look around, confused.

The couple moves under a streetlight and for a second is in full view. There's Zack, walking along and putting his cell phone up to his ear. And in my ear I hear his voice.

"Hello?" Beside him, just inches away as he talks to me on his cell, her hand tucked into the crook of his elbow, stands Rosie.

I don't stop to think. In a few giant steps, I run across Carousel Avenue, out onto the Seawalk, and straight into their little circle of light.

"*You!*" I push Zack in the chest, hard, with the palms of both hands, sending him reeling backward a step. Rosie cries out and stretches a steadying hand to Zack, which infuriates me.

"Zack chose *me! I'm* his girl—not you!"

At the same time, Zack says "Alex, you don't understand!"

"I know what I see!"

"If you'll just calm down, I can explain."

"Don't bother!" I turn and run. My legs moving as fast they can take me, I burst through my front door a minute later and throw myself on my bed. The house is quiet, my mom fast asleep. My breath comes in painful gasps, and my throat feels raw. I lie there in the dark on my side with my knees curled up to my chest.

In the other room, I hear my cell phone ring, then go to voice mail. I know it's Zack, calling to beg for forgiveness. I won't answer it. It's over.

I lie there for a while, my thoughts flitting from one depressing subject to the next. Not only will I spend my life slaving over wedding cakes on a small island, but I'll be a dried up old spinster, too. I'll live with my mother until she dies, after which I'll get a cat or a parakeet. I'll never find a man. I'll be the world's oldest living virgin.

A hand knocks on the door. I lift my head up from the bedspread, feeling hopeful in spite of myself. Zack's actually come over to apologize.

I crawl out of bed and stumble to the front door. He must feel really bad about what he did. I can at least see what he has to say. I reach the door and stop to smooth my hair a little. Then I open it.

There, standing under the naked bulb of our porch light, is Rosie.

• • •

She wears a pale yellow summer dress with a soft, billowy skirt and little flats. The yellow sets off her dark skin and eyes. Her nails are manicured and painted coral, her hair is thick and straight and perfect, and her arms are crossed on her chest, her foot tapping impatiently. She is beautiful and primed for battle.

I stop short, suddenly nervous.

"Can I come in?" Her voice is cool and detached. "This won't take long."

I'm sure I have bedspread marks on my face. I blow my nose into the remnants of tissue in my hand. It makes an embarrassing honk.

"Okay. My mom's asleep, though, so we have to keep our voices down." I wave her into my living room, thinking how shabby it must look to her. In addition to owning large tracts of land on the island, the Martinezes own some of the businesses on Carousel

Avenue. They live in a fancy house on the side of Mt. Vazquez, below the Inn.

She doesn't waste any time. "Zack didn't lie to you tonight. He was helping his Dad move some things into their garage. But when I called him around nine, he was done, so I talked him into meeting me."

"Meeting you? Why?" Anger curls its way through me. Why won't she leave him alone? He's told her he wants to be with me.

"I wanted to see him just one last time." For a split second, Rosie's calm surface tears open and reveals the pain underneath, shining through her eyes. Then she closes up again. "To get a few things off my chest."

Oh, right, closure. But I get it. I know what loss and disappointment feel like.

"Why are you here? You don't think he can speak for himself to tell me what happened?"

"Well, it's not like you were letting him get a word in *edgewise*." Rosie purses her lips as if she's exasperated. "But, no, that's not why I came. I just want to say something to you."

"Okay." Unexpectedly, dread rises up in me.

Rosie fastens a glare on me. "You got him. Now *don't hurt him.* Cuz if you do, I swear...." Her face is a thunderstorm.

She's got a lot of nerve. "I have no intention of hurting him," I say. "You have no reason to think I would!"

She raises an eyebrow. "Oh, I don't?" We glare at each other. "Everybody knows you're out of here, Alex. The first scholarship, the first offer from some Ivy League school, and you'll be gone." She looks me directly in the eyes. "Tell me it's not true."

I try. I try to say it's not true, but I can't choke the words out. Of course, it's true. If I got the chance and felt that Mom would be okay, I'd be gone. I'd leave the island, my mother, and my home. I'd leave Zack.

What does that say about me? That I don't really love Zack? That I'm not ready for love?

"I knew it!" she says. "You don't have any real loyalty to him."

"We're not ready for commitments like that!"

She shakes her head. "*You're* not ready. But Zack and I both know what we want. Our lives are on this island. We're good for each other."

Impatience floods me. "You're just mad because he chose me!"

She looks at me pityingly. "Zack holds onto things. He's still hanging onto this old idea of his that he'd always be with you."

I have to admit, she knows how Zack's mind works. An ocean liner changes direction faster than he does. Still, I argue with her. "Well, what's wrong with that?"

"What wrong with it is that you don't feel the same way. You just said you'd leave him if something better came along." Rosie pins me down with a firm look. "And I'm saying, don't you dare think you can play around with him and then take off. Because, me and Zack, we could have something *really good* together."

"Are you done now?" I'd eat ground glass before I'd admit to her that maybe she's got a point.

"Yes." She stands up, smoothing her skirt, and lets herself out the front door.

I sit there alone on our sagging couch. I can hear Zack talking about Rosie. *I did really like her.* About me, he had said, *I've always pictured myself with you. We've always been together.* Not exactly a ringing declaration of passion.

And how do I feel? I'll always love Zack, but if I knew Mom would be okay, I'd leave him for a college degree and a career. Am I just clinging to Zack in case I end up stuck here, unable to go? He deserves better than that.

But Zack's the only good thing in my life right now—the only good thing in my future, for that matter. My eyes are throbbing and my head's pounding. I curl up on top of my bedspread, still in my clothes, and lie there for a long time until I fall asleep.

Chapter Twenty-Six

Left. Right. Left. Right. My feet press against the pedals of my mountain bike, propelling it up the steep fire road to the top of Mt. Alejandro. Sweat drips down my chin and onto my thighs. My breathing rasps raggedly in and out.

My mind's a crazy quilt of impressions and feelings. Hope, that somehow I'll achieve my goals in life. Anger, that Mom holds on to me and keeps me back. Fear that, to fulfill my dreams, I'll have to desert my mother. I don't want to have to make that choice.

Left. Right. Left. Right. My brain spins faster than the wheels of my bike as it tries to sort out the mess that is my life. With Zack around, at least I'm not alone here. I have a friend—more than that, a partner—someone who'll stand by me.

Memories of me and Zack flash through my mind: a lifetime spent together— our dives, skateboarding to school, the games of beach volleyball. He's not just my past; he's my only shot at a future if I stay on this island.

I keep pedaling, driving my feet around and around. I'm not sure why, but I need to reach the top of the mountain, to see as far as I can.

When I get there, I jump off my bike, letting it fall over on the grass, and run to the cliff edge. This is where Zack and I stood on the day we decided to be together. That day, I was happy, thinking that at least one thing was going my way.

What's wrong with me, that it's not enough to just stay on Santa Rita with Zack, when I love him, and I love the island, too? Yet Rosie's right. If I got the chance to go to school, I'd take it.

Is it fair to Zack to choose him by default?

I look out toward the mainland, clearly outlined today on the horizon. It's not that far away. The almost vertical rock walls beneath me plunge down to the water. This water, this Pacific Ocean that surrounds my island home, extends thousands of miles to touch places I've never gone, but long to see someday.

A breeze blows through my hair and cools my face. The part of me that's stubborn and determined gives a sharp kick to the part of me that feels sorry for myself. I've just had a couple of setbacks, that's all.

I've stuck to my plan, and there's no reason it can't work. My research is right on schedule. Mom was getting better after the fire. I'll keep working with her, help her become more independent.

There are a lot of *maybe's* in my future, but *maybe* means there's hope. Once again the little refrain that I've heard before picks up in my head. *I can do it.*

My breathing back to normal now, I get my bike off the grass and head down the steep slope toward home. As my wheels start to turn, grief hits me. I'll have to say goodbye to Zack. It hurts to think of it. Why does doing the right thing—and I know I am— make me feel so bad?

Left, right, left, right. The pedals fly around without resistance, now that I'm going downhill. My heart starts to pound, and my breathing deepens. As usual, movement seems to make things better. I can see every leaf on the trees, hear every bird chirp, feel the blood surging through my veins and arteries.

Focus on what's good—the research I'll do, the scholarship I'll get, the chance that maybe Mom will be okay by herself and I can go to a great college, one I actually want to attend, rather than the one that's closest.

I can do it. I can do it. I can do it.

My legs pick up the rhythm that takes me safely down the mountain and home.

• • •

Zack and I lie on our backs on the air mattress in his truck, not touching, but instead talking and looking up at the night sky. I'm filled with a weird happy-sad feeling: happy that Zack and I will always be friends and sad because that's all we'll ever be.

"One thing," I tell Zack. "You've still gotta partner me on my research dives."

"Done."

"Will Rosie let you out?" I tease him, poking his leg with my toe.

"Rosie ain't the boss o' me." He pokes my leg in return. "Anyway, she thinks you're cool."

I snort. "Yeah, right."

"No, she does. She thinks you kick ass."

"I have a feeling Rosie kicks some pretty good ass herself." Rosie's okay, I've decided. If Zack's not going to be with me, she's a darn good alternative.

I'm doing the right thing—I know I am. But inside, I quiver. I'm walking away from the best thing in my life right now, with no guarantees to take its place.

Appreciate what you've got, I tell myself. But I don't know if I can. It seems like this is just the way I'm hard-wired. No matter what happens, I'm destined to always want more than I have.

• • •

When I get home that night, Mom's waiting up for me. "Do you want some tea?" she asks. "It's decaffeinated."

"Sure." I'm surprised. She's barely spoken to me since my fiasco of a lunch with Lester.

"Let's go out back," she says, and we head out to sit in the rickety lawn chairs that wobble on the uneven concrete surface of our back patio. I've barely sat down when Mom starts in.

"Am I really that bad?"

Startled, I dodge away from a genuine answer. "C'mon, Mom!"

"No, Alex, I'm serious. You should have heard how critical Lester was. I've been thinking about it ever since." Mom clears her throat and holds her tea in both hands. She hasn't taken a sip yet. "Is he right? Am I really that awful?"

I lick my lips. "Well, it would be nice if you'd support me more. Help me get some of the things I want."

"Like what?"

"I'd like to travel off the island sometimes." I take a deep breath. "And ... go away to college."

She deflates in front of my eyes, getting small and scared looking. "I can see that you would," she says in a tiny voice. 'Lester says I make you work too much. Is that true?"

I hadn't foreseen how hard it would be to tell Mom how I feel, knowing how unhappy it makes her. I choke out an answer. "I don't mind long hours, but I don't want to make wedding cakes my whole life. And I'd like to be paid for my work."

For a minute, the old mom emerges. "Anything else? Maybe a free trip around the world?"

I just look at her, and after a minute, she looks down, shamefaced. "Sorry."

"It's okay."

Her mouth works as her eyes go glassy. "Alex? I never meant to hurt you."

"I know." My throat aches. I take a sip of tea, which is cold by now.

"Will you forgive me?" Her cheeks are red and blotchy, and she dabs at her nose with a tissue.

"Of course I forgive you. I was part of what happened."

"Lester's coming out to visit tomorrow. It may be the last time I see him." Her eyes are large and frightened.

181

"If he's coming to you, it's because he's still trying to make it work with you. Why not just listen to him, tell him how you feel, and try to compromise?" I want her to be happy. Not just for my sake, but for hers. I remember how Rosie had put it. *Something really good.* Mom and Lester could have something really good together.

A line of doubt creases her forehead. "I have to convince Lester that I sincerely want to change. He says I have to prove it to him." She droops and presses her lips into a tight line.

"How?"

She considers it. "I think if I did something for you, that might work."

Her forehead crinkles even more as she focuses on the problem. "Is there something that you want, Alex? Something I could do for you right now, so I could show Lester I'm serious?"

Is she doing this for my sake, or Lester's? Do I even care, if it means I can have something that's important to me, something I thought was completely unattainable? And I know exactly what it is, too.

"Well," I say, "I could use three days off. Over Labor Day." Ignoring her startled, you've-got-to-be-kidding-me expression, I go on to explain. "You see, there's this party…."

• • •

In six days Jeremy will leave. He has stayed on Santa Rita as long as he possibly could. He'll spend just a week at home in Beverly Hills, then head for Stanford. I can't believe how much I'll miss him.

He's standing in our tiny dining room holding a carton of eggs. He's decided that since he learned to dive here, he should also, before his departure, learn to make a wedding cake.

Knowing that he's grown up surrounded by nannies and housekeepers, I ask him, "Can you do *anything* in a kitchen?" I reach

182

for a large mixing bowl. We're going to make four round layers of coconut cake.

He points to the carton in his hand. "I happen to be a master egg cracker."

I give him a couple of bowls, then begin sifting the dry ingredients together. Jeremy cracks eggs into the large mixing bowl and places the shells in the smaller one. "Hey, keep an eye on your mail," he says. "You're getting an invitation."

"To what?"

"To Gramps's birthday party on Labor Day." He empties another egg into the bowl with a flourish.

"I asked Mom, but she hasn't told me yet if she's worked things out."

"Gram and Gramps really want you there."

"Well, unless I clone myself or an angel falls from the sky to help Mom, I have to be here that weekend. We'll see." I hope it works out. I would love to see the Broadmans and visit their home.

We mix together the wet and dry cake ingredients, pour the mixture into pans, and put the pans in the oven. "Time to make frosting," I say.

"It's nice to have you to myself again," Jeremy says. "For a while there, you were spending so much time with Zack that I was forced to go hang with Rebecca."

"Forced? I thought you had *abandoned* me for Rebecca." I reach for the butter and cream cheese, which have been softening in a bowl, and start creaming them with the mixer.

"What could possibly give you that idea?" Jeremy carries bowls and spatulas to the kitchen and loading them into the dishwasher, one of the skills he picked up this summer at Dizzy's.

Now that he's asked, I'm not sure. "But she's such an incredible singer!"

"Well, yeah, it's fun to sing with her. But that girl operates on a frequency all her own."

"Oh." I feel like a feather about to float away on a breeze. Rebecca *is* incredibly talented. I have warm and charitable feelings towards her. I stop the mixer, making my voice resound in the sudden silence. We've been almost yelling at each other over the machine.

"Alex?" Jeremy says. His smile vanishes, and he picks at some cake batter that's stuck to his shirt.

"Yes?" I begin stirring powdered sugar into the cream cheese and butter.

"Be my friend? Always?"

I stop stirring. "Of course I will!"

He studies the counter as if something desperately important is engraved there. "No, I mean it. Because you're special to me."

I touch his hand lightly. "I mean it, too."

He smiles, pleased, then looks at me with the most tender expression in his eyes. "I need to tell you something." His face darkens. "This is huge for me, okay?"

The kitchen goes quiet. "Okay," I answer. We sit down on the chairs at the tiny kitchen table, facing each other. Questions run through my head. What's he going to say to me? Does Jeremy feel something for me? Is that why he looks at me the way he does?

"Remember how I said Jennifer and I had a fight before she left for New York?"

I nod.

"She was going to leave in a few days, to start her internship." He takes a deep breath. "We went out, and she told me she wanted to have sex with me, that she was finally ready for it. She had brought condoms and everything."

He looks so miserable I think he's going to stop telling his story. But, he goes on. "So, here she was, all ready to go. But I wasn't. I didn't—couldn't—do it. And she got pissed off at me. And you know what she said?"

I can hardly look at Jeremy's eyes, they're so haunted.

"She said 'Emma told me you were gay, but I wouldn't believe her!' And it turned out they'd made a bet. Jennifer bet she could get me to have sex with her, and Emma bet it wouldn't happen. So I guess Jenn told Emma she'd won the bet."

Jeremy's gay? At the same time that I feel a twist of disappointment in my stomach, something else clicks quietly into place for me, this feeling of, *Okay, I get it now.* With Zack, there was a pull, a spark, that made me feel sexy. But Jeremy's like my favorite pair of old jeans—reliable and comfortable.

My mind jumps to Fritz and Maurice, the two old cowboys who live down the street and who run the horse stable outside of town. They give riding lessons and organize hayrides for the tourists during the summer. When they got unofficially married last year, we not only attended the event, but as our gift to them, made their wedding cake—a fantastic tiered concoction decorated in lavender, pink and silver with two horse-riding cowboys on top.

But maybe Jeremy's jumping to conclusions. He sits hunched over, his elbows on his knees. I pull my chair over and sit next to him, squeezing his shoulder. We both have flour on our hands and clothes, and I'm just making it worse, smearing it everywhere.

"Those girls are brats! I mean, I know Emma's your sister, but that was *rotten*! And anyway, just because you couldn't have sex with a girl one time doesn't make you gay."

When he doesn't say anything, I go on, "Maybe you just need to meet the right girl."

Jeremy's shaking his head. "That's not gonna work."

"How do you know that?"

"Because I've met the right girl, and I'm still gay."

I'm confused. "I hope I'm not being too pushy, but Jennifer does not sound like the right girl for you."

He shakes his head. "It's not Jennifer." He's giving me that look again, that sad look of longing. "The thing with Emma and Jennifer happened just a few weeks before Caroline's wedding. I was dying to get away from my family for the summer, so I could get some perspective and think. I knew Santa Rita was the perfect place the minute I saw it."

He's looking increasingly nervous, glancing at the floor, then over at me, then back to the floor. "Then I met you, and I thought, *Damn! If there was ever a girl I could want, it would be her!*"

185

My mouth falls open. No sound comes out. I can't even imagine what to say.

He goes on. "So I came out here for the summer. And I've loved every minute. And now I know for sure I'm gay."

My lips tremble. "So being with me turned you gay?" I'm trying to hold together the emotional dam that's keeping back hurt and embarrassment.

"It's not like that! You're so amazing and beautiful, Alex. If I can't be attracted to you, I must be gay."

"And you don't want to be?" I jump up and walk over to the frosting bowl on the counter.

He follows me. "Hell, no. Although, I think I've always known. But when you don't want something to be true, you find a way to ignore it, to make it go away."

I nod, listening to him and trying to imagine how he feels. "So what are you going to do now?"

"Tell my family." His voice is hollow. "That's another reason I came out here. To think about when and how to tell them." He sighs. "It's not gonna be pretty."

"They'll stand by you. You're wonderful, Jeremy. They know that."

"Thanks. I wish I could be so sure."

As for me, *I* wish I could erase the sadness from his face. The bowl of frosting's on the counter in front of me. I take a finger full and flick it at him. It lands on his shirt sleeve.

The sparkle returns to his eyes. He gives me an evil grin. "Watch out!"

I load up with another finger full, but Jeremy has grabbed the spray hose from the sink and stands his ground, aiming it straight at me.

I make my face look innocent. "We can't mess up the kitchen. Mom'll kill me."

"All right." Jeremy replaces the spray hose in its holder.

I hurl a dollop of frosting in his direction, laughter bubbling up at the expression on his face. The frosting hits his belt buckle.

With a yell, Jeremy attacks, grabbing me with one hand and scooping a handful of frosting with the other.

I shriek. The fight is on. It only lasts a few minutes, but we end up on the floor, my hair full of frosting, and Jeremy with a good cup of it down the inside of his shirtfront. I can't stop laughing. It feels wonderful to laugh like that, spontaneous laughter that comes from deep inside and fills my whole body.

Jeremy's examining his expensive watch, now encrusted with frosting. Fortunately, he's laughing, too.

"I'm sorry," I say.

"It'll clean up." He scrapes at the watch with a fingernail. "I think." Still on the floor, we lean against the cabinets together, my sticky head on his shoulder.

"I wish you weren't leaving, Jeremy. I'm going to miss you so much!" In a few months, everything has shifted for me. I still have a best friend, but after all these years, it isn't Zack anymore.

"I'm going to miss you, too," he says. "And I'll miss this place. It's funny—this little island of yours? It really grows on you."

• • •

I meet with Roy in his living room to update him about my research project. His two boys thunder in and out, simulating machine guns.

"I'll be diving to collect samples for my study. Zack will partner me on the dives."

"What about funding?"

"I have enough money set aside." I show him my list of equipment needed and its cost.

A three-year old warrior leaps into his lap, and Roy folds his arms around him. "Fantastic. Have you prepared a timeline?"

"Working on it. I'll have the final plan for you by Labor Day." I leave him, my head spinning with ideas.

It's going to happen. I'm going to do this project, and it's going to jumpstart me into scholarship money. Now I've really got to get

Mom up on her own two feet. But with my project falling into place, anything seems possible.

When I enter our kitchen, Mom's doing one of her experimental cake edgings, a stunning band of red, black, and yellow shapes that my eyes see as abstract at first, but then break down into a repeating pattern of hearts, spades, clubs, and diamonds, along with the kings and queens of playing cards.

"The clients are professional poker players," she says. "They want a gambling cake. The layers are going to be rectangular, like playing cards."

"It's really cool, Mom."

"They flipped for this pattern when I showed it to them. Can you imagine? At first, they wanted a cake shaped like a pile of dice!" Her lip curls.

Feeling a surge of love for her, I make a horrified face. "That's terrible!"

Laughing, she snaps a towel at me. "It's important to do these things right, you know."

"Absolutely!" My mom's cakes are phenomenal. Some, like this, are one-of-a-kind.

I get how she feels, I realize suddenly. For me, it's not about wedding cakes. But it's the same thing. The drive to do what you love, and do it well.

I guess I got it from her.

Chapter Twenty-Seven

It's Jeremy's last evening on the island. We take a final stroll along the Seawalk together.

"Aren't you excited?" I ask him. "To go off to college?" His life seems so perfect to me. I'd give anything to know that, a year from now, I'd be taking off for Stanford.

He shrugs. "First, I've gotta face the lions in their den."

I know how nervous Jeremy is about telling his family he's gay.

"Who knows?" he jokes. "If my family throws me out of the house, I may be back here in a few days!"

"They wouldn't do that." We stop to lean against the railing and watch a speedboat slice through the water. Behind it, a parasailor rises into the air, spreading its wings of brilliant blue, red, and green.

"I'm not even sure I'd mind," he says.

"What do you mean?"

"Well, I don't want my family mad at me, but I'm not feeling this whole college thing, you know?" He looks over at me to gauge my reaction.

"But ... *Stanford!* Don't you want to go?"

His hands are tight on the railing. "It's weird. It's like... I'm not ready."

I start to speak, but my cell phone cuts me off.

"Alex? It's Lester. Sue's here with me on the speaker phone." Lester's staying in his old room at the Seashell, working things out with Mom. They haven't said much about it, but at least he's still here.

"Hi honey!" Mom's voice carols out of the receiver.

"Hi! What's up?" I can't imagine why they're calling.

Lester gets right to the point. "Sue says you had an invitation for Labor Day. For Edward Broadman's birthday party?"

"Yeah, I did." I signal madly to Jeremy, making faces to indicate that something's up. He moves in, trying to listen through my receiver.

"We think you ought to go. I'll help Sue with the cakes."

Stunned, I hold my phone so Jeremy can listen too. "But, can the two of you manage? It's a lot!"

"I think so," Mom says. "If you do the planning and prep work, Lester does the driving, lifting and carrying, and I do the cake assembly, it should work out."

"You guys would do that for me? Lester, you'd give up your Labor Day weekend?"

"Of course," Lester answers. "Sue has to work anyway, and I'm happy if I'm with her. So go to your party—it sounds like a good one."

"Thank you both so much." Then a thought occurs to me. "Is it too late to say yes?" I ask Jeremy.

"You're already on the list," he answers, smugly.

"You knew?" I make an outraged face at him.

"We called him yesterday," Mom says. She must have overheard me talking to him. "Just to ask if the invitation was still open."

"Gram and Gramps are expecting you," Jeremy confirms.

I thank Mom and Lester again and hang up. My brain shifts into overdrive. What will I wear, how will I get there? I'll sell some more diving equipment to pay my expenses.

"Thank God you're coming," Jeremy says. "I think the average age at this party's gonna be sixty-five. Gramps said to tell you

190

there'll be someone there he wants you to meet. I think it's an old college friend of his. From Princeton."

"Princeton!" There's a school I could never attend. They'd probably never accept me. Even if they did, it's three thousand miles away from Mom. And I'd have to go into debt for the rest of my life to pay for it.

But I have to ask. "Why does he want me to talk to this Princeton guy?"

"I wasn't really listening," Jeremy confesses. "I think he has career advice for you."

"Okay." I can't see what this man would have to say to me, but I'd be happy to find out.

A car will pick me up at the boat terminal on Saturday of Labor Day weekend and bring me to the Broadman home. After the bigger party on Sunday, there'll be a small family brunch on Monday.

"Oh, Jeremy, this is *great!*" I clasp my hands together, as if in prayer.

He wears a smile that seems to come straight from his heart. "You're like a little kid, you know? I haven't seen you this excited since you found that free lotion in the hotel bathroom."

"Don't make fun of me!" I put my hands on my hips.

"Never." He looks around him. "This summer's been great. I love this place. And you know what else? I think I like the restaurant business. I could really see getting into that, as a complement to the family business." He puts one foot on the railing, leaning forward to watch the glass-bottom boat troll by with its load of tourists.

Jeremy has never mentioned his family's business before. All I know is what that guy, Tom, on the boat said. "Do you really own half of Orange County?" I venture to ask as we head back in the direction of my house.

"Nah." Jeremy shakes his head in amusement. "We own hotels."

Hotels? I have a sudden memory of the beautiful hotel at Disneyland where we stayed.

"Yes." He answers my unspoken question. "We own that hotel. Along with ... a few others."

"A few?"

"Well, more than a few," Jeremy admits. "We own the Empress Resort Hotels."

The Disneyland Empress. The card in the hotel room had said there were a hundred seventy Empress luxury hotels around the world.

"Wow." The Broadman lifestyle is beyond anything I could ever imagine.

We've reached my house. My heart is tearing slowly apart at the thought of him leaving.

We don't speak. He crushes me in his arms, and we stay that way for a long moment.

Finally, he lets go. "I'll call you. Every day."

"You better," I say.

He walks away fast before I can say anything else.

Chapter Twenty-Eight

I'm sitting on my living room sofa with my feet pulled up under me. My completed, final research plan is in a fat binder in my lap. It rocks. It has all the components: objectives, materials, methodology—I can hardly wait to show it to Roy.

Lester and Mom walk in. I haven't seen them much since Lester started coming out here again, but my mom had called to say they were "working things out." Lester has extended his stay for several days, but will be going home tomorrow. Now, as he and Mom enter the living room, they're holding hands, talking excitedly back and forth.

"Shall we show her?" Lester asks Mom.

"Why not?" My mother waltzes across the living room, her left hand held out in front of her. "Look!" She wears a small diamond on her ring finger. "We bought it at The Jewel Box. We're getting married!"

In shock, I get to my feet. I take my mother's hand, looking at her ring. "It's beautiful. Omigod, this is fantastic!" Lester's eyes meet mine for a moment, while his lips form the words "Thank you." I shake my head. I'm the one who should be thanking him.

I have a sudden thought. "Lester, what about your wife?" That seems like a problem to me.

"My divorce was finalized last week," he says.

My mind runs like a racehorse. This will solve all my problems. Lester can help my mom with the business, leaving me to spend my last year at Paradise High, doing my research project and applying to colleges. And scholarships. I can leave Santa Rita in a year, knowing Mom will be all right—happy, in fact. Everything is perfect.

"We're getting married this fall," Mom is saying. "We just have to find the venue."

"That shouldn't be hard. We know every venue on the island," I say.

She and Lester exchange glances. "We'll probably get married on the mainland," my mom tells me, "closer to home." Mom sits down on the arm chair across from me, prim, with her feet together, while Lester stands behind her, his hand on the back of the chair. His nose is sunburned, and his hair stands up in little wisps on his head.

"Home?" I repeat.

"Alex," Lester says, "I need to live in Los Angeles, where my clients are. Sue has agreed to move there." He watches me carefully.

"But I still have a year of high school left!"

"The timing's not great," Mom says. "But we'll find you a really terrific school, so you can enjoy your senior year." As she speaks, she holds her hand out in front of her, admiring her ring.

I wanted to leave, but not now. Not this way. I'm supposed to throw my research project down the drain? Spend my senior year as a newcomer in a strange place, far from everyone I know?

"I need to be here next year."

My mom voice hardens. "Alex, we can't just leave you behind."

"Sure you can. I'll be eighteen!"

"And you think you're going to live out here by yourself? How are you going to pay your expenses?"

"I'll figure something out!"

Mom throws her hands up in frustration and jumps to her feet, her face turning red. We glare at each other.

Lester slides a hand around Mom's waist. "Easy does it, beautiful," he says in a good-natured, teasing way.

In an instant, she transforms, relaxing and taking a deep breath.

"Let's take some time to think about it," Lester says. He gives me a wink as he stands there in our living room, his knobby, freckled knees protruding from his shorts. "I don't know what the answer is, but as Alex puts it, we'll figure something out."

"You're right, Lester! Alex, we'll talk about it." Mom exchanges a smoldering look with her man.

"Okay," I say, too surprised to say anything else.

Is it possible that Lester Lindstrom, the accountant from Burbank, can work miracles? Can Lester salvage my senior year of high school?

If not, I think, it doesn't matter. Because I will.

• • •

As I arrive for dinner at Jenna and Dizzy's house, Jenna chops vegetables along to country music. On the kitchen table near a cutting board lie an avocado and some hard-boiled eggs, while a large bowl holds already-cut tomato, ham, lettuce, cucumber, carrot and chunks of cheese. She's making her Chop-Til-You-Drop Chopped Salad.

I've come to ask if they'll take me in this fall after Mom leaves.

They have to do it. I won't be any trouble. I'll sleep on the futon and do dishes and housework to earn my keep. They won't even know I'm there.

"It's too hot to cook," Jenna says, whacking at a radish.

"Never mind that you work up a sweat chopping all that stuff." Dizzy hands her a tall glass of iced water.

Jenna laughs, stopping to take a sip. She has tied up her long hair in a knot on the top of her head and wears a loose, sleeveless dress. Although she's gained a little weight, she looks beautiful, her skin glowing like the inside of a seashell, in translucent pinks and peaches.

As she begins to set the table, Dizzy jumps to his feet, taking the plates from her hands. "I'll do that," he says. "You rest."

"Okay." She sinks down into a chair. "Might as well let him spoil me," she says, a little smile tucked into the corners of her mouth.

I'm going to wait until dinner to give them the news of Sue's engagement to Lester. When they hear the plans for me, they'll offer me their home—I know it. They'll want me to stay with them.

Dizzy and Jenna whisper to each other. "Shall we tell her?" Dizzy asks Jenna.

"Tell me what?"

"It's a miracle!" Jenna says. "I can't believe it." She pauses for effect. "*I'm pregnant!*"

I catch my breath for a second, then let out a yell that could scare the sea life all the way down to Baja. "That's wonderful! I thought you'd given up!"

Jenna's pretty old—almost forty. "We had," she said. "But, God had other plans for us!" Her eyes mist over. "We waited as long as we could before telling people. You know…. to be on the safe side."

"When are you due?" I clutch Dizzy's arm in congratulations, thrilled for them, even though a corner of my mind is beginning to recognize what this means for me.

"January 10."

"I'm so glad for you." I mean it, but a pocket of sadness opens up in me, knowing I can never stay with them now.

Dizzy orders Jenna to stay seated while he finishes setting the table and serves up the dinner. "No point in taking chances," he says.

"All these years and now, all of a sudden, you'd think I was a china doll, about to break," Jenna complains in a happy voice.

"How long have you guys known each other?" I know Jenna was raised on the island, but Dizzy came over when he was older.

"First time I came out here, I was eighteen," Dizzy says. "But I didn't meet Jenna for a few years."

196

"That's cuz when you were eighteen, I was fourteen," she retorts.

"Good thing I didn't know you then," Dizzy jokes. "I never *could* keep my hands offa you." The phone rings, and he goes to answer it. "Okay, see you tomorrow." He hangs up.

"Zack," he says.

"Him and Rosie?"

"Going strong," Jenna says.

I try to keep my face calm and untroubled, but a thin needle of pain shoots through me. Since Zack and Rosie got back together, it's been pretty clear.

All those two needed was for me to get out of the way.

I don't mind, I insist to myself. I'm focused on the Broadmans' party and starting my research this fall. Which, somehow, I *will* do.

"We just want both you and Zack to be happy," Jenna says. "You mean so much to us." We've finished our salads. Jenna gets up and opens the freezer. "Ice cream?"

We take our bowls outside to the little back yard, which is big enough to hold three lawn chairs.

"Zack's probably a lot happier with Rosie than he would have been with me." Feeling moody, I plunge my spoon into the ice cream.

"It's *your* happiness we've been worried about," Dizzy says in a mild tone, settling into a lawn chair. Despite his cheerful temperament, he has the sad, soulful eyes of a Basset hound. He has pistachio ice cream on his mustache. Jenna reaches out with a napkin and wipes it off.

"Me? Why?"

"Zack's different from you." Dizzy says, "He's a Santa Rita boy."

First Rosie, now him. Why does everyone keep saying things like that?

I jump to my feet, making them both draw back in surprise. "I *love* Santa Rita! I'll *always* come back to this place!"

"Right," Dizzy says. "You'll always *come back.*"

I stare at him, taking in his meaning.

Jenna leans forward. "Alex," she says in a gentle voice, "this island's too small for you. You need to open up your wings and fly!"

I might as well tell them now. "Speaking of leaving the island, I have news, too," I say. And I tell them, standing on their back step while they sit in their lawn chairs.

"*Now?*" Jenna's voice scales up in distress. "Oh, honey, before your last year of school? How do you feel about that?"

"Bad," I admit. "But I don't know what to do about it."

I can almost hear their thoughts. *She could have stayed with us, but there's the baby now.*

Their unhappy silence says it all.

Chapter Twenty-Nine

I pack and repack my overnight bag for the Broadmans' party. It's weird leaving with everything so up in the air: we haven't decided where I'll be living and going to school this fall.

But, for me, a small green leaf has sprouted, and the leaf is hope. I've had another idea, my best one yet. I've been staying up at night to make lists and crunch numbers. I haven't told anyone, but the more I think about it, the more possible it seems. To put it all together, I just have to put one key piece into place. This weekend, at the party.

Despite the geriatric guest list, I want to look good. The whole weekend will be casual, with swimming and time spent outdoors, so I pack two bathing suits, three combinations of shorts with cute tops, two sundresses, sneakers and sandals. Then I take them all out and try them on, checking the top half of me in my bureau mirror and climbing up on a chair to see the bottom half. The clothes look nice, but no different than the last few times I checked them in the mirror. I repack them, zip my bag, and tell myself, *That's it. You're ready to go.*

Lester's coming tomorrow to help Mom over Labor Day, then staying on, because Jessica's wedding is the following weekend. We're all excited about it, and about Mom and Lester's wedding, too. The only sore point, the thing that's hanging out there unresolved, is the pesky subject of Alexandra.

My eighteenth birthday is the weekend after Jessica's wedding. "Alex, Lester wants me to come to a Lindstrom family reunion that weekend," Mom tells me. "You're invited, too, of course. We'll have a birthday party for you."

"Do I have to?"

"Don't you want to celebrate your birthday?"

"It doesn't have to be on the exact day. We'll figure something out." We keep saying that, but we never do.

No matter. I know what I want and, for the first time in my life, I know how to get it. This time, maybe, just maybe, I'll be able to take control of my life and start to live it. My way.

• • •

I look around as I walk down the gangplank of the Traveler and into the Long Beach terminal, my overnight bag on my shoulder. I'm wearing a cute t-shirt and some matching shorts, with my hair tied up in a ponytail. Jeremy has said a driver will meet me, but it hasn't occurred to me to ask how the driver and I are supposed to find each other.

A large dark-skinned man in a uniform steps forward, holding a sign that says, "Marshall."

"Oh, hi! That's me!" I squeak, completely intimidated.

He gives me a kindly smile full of gold crowns, takes my bag, and leads me out to the longest, blackest car I've ever seen, opening the back door and helping me inside. I find myself alone in a space big enough to accommodate an inflatable dinghy, if I'd felt the need to bring one along. A glass partition separates me from the driver in the front seat.

I'm way too excited to sit here by myself. I knock on the partition, and it rolls open.

"Hi," I say. "Is this a limousine?" From watching TV, I know it is, but somehow I have to ask.

"It sure is, young lady." His voice is a dark, deep rumble, with a Southern twang to it.

"My name's Alex."

"Now, how come a pretty girl like you has a boy's name?"

"Well, it's Alexandra."

"Pleased to meet you, Miss Alexandra. I'm Luther. Luther Hawks."

"Hi." There's a moment of silence, while I sink into the soft leather seat.

"Miss Alexandra, I'm gonna drive you up to the Broadmans' now."

I can't see him, but his deep voice rolls easily through the opening. "But I'm gonna leave this thing here open, in case you have any more questions, okay?"

"Thank you," I say, in a tiny voice.

The limo doesn't so much roll as float away from the terminal. I'd be in heaven if I weren't so worried about Jeremy. He's been right to fear his family's reaction to his announcement.

"Mom shut herself up in her bedroom, and Dad took off in his car," he told me after his first day back, his voice sounding thin and scared over the phone. "And *my sister*, well, you can imagine. Emma's been on the phone all evening, probably telling the news services."

"What about your grandparents?" I hardly dare ask the question.

"They know. But they haven't mentioned it to me." I've never heard Jeremy sound so lost. There's been no progress to report since then. And tomorrow's Edward's big birthday celebration with the entire family.

• • •

When Luther opens the door of the car for me, Jeremy's waiting. He laughs as he picks me up and swings me around.

"*Jeremy!* I'm so glad to see you!"

201

He sets me down, holding me at the waist to steady me, while I try to focus my eyes on the sight in front of me. I have the impression of steps, a wide veranda, columns, impossibly high ceilings, and a gleaming door opening in front of me.

"I have to talk to you," I say in his ear.

"She's here!" Jeremy calls out as Edward Broadman appears, followed by Margaret. As my feet touch the marble floor of their entryway, I hear Mom's voice in my ear. *You'll never fit into their world.*

As the Wedding Cake Girl, I never even fit into my own world, now that I think of it. It's like the killer whales that are trained to do tricks in captivity. I've always loved the beautiful black and white creatures, but felt sorry for them, too—kept in a place they were never meant to live doing things they were never meant to do.

Maybe Mom's right that I'm a misfit at this party. I barely know these people. And they barely know me. The one and only time I've seen them, I was a worker bee at their event, doing a job for pay. I know what those rules for behavior are. But here, now, invited as a close friend of *this* family? Although I think of them by their first names, I could never address them that way.

I move forward. "Mr. Broadman, Mrs. Broadman... it's so good to see you again."

"And it's so lovely to see you." She wears a tailored red skirt, white blouse, and black cardigan and feels small in my arms, as I stoop to hug her. "We are so *delighted* you came!"

"Welcome!" Edward shakes my hand, his blue eyes warm in greeting, but observant, too, as if he sees and understands everything about me. "I hear that you and Jeremy have become friends!"

"Yes. We have." I'm horrified to hear an edge in my voice, which I didn't intend at all, but which says *yeah, and I'm on his side no matter what.* I peek up through my eyelashes at Edward, fearing his disapproval, but am met instead with a thoughtful look.

"I'll take you to your room." Margaret chats to me as we walk. "So many of the guests tomorrow are our age, but we will have some younger people as well. We'll make sure you get introduced, and we'll have swimming and other activities."

As we walk, I glimpse large airy rooms; lush fabrics; bay windows full of light; the textures of porcelain, crystal, velvet, cherrywood and satin; subtle wallpapers; and perfectly chosen splashes of color.

It could be a museum or a five-star hotel just as well as someone's home. It's enormous, going on for room after room.

Margaret leads me to a door, which opens to show the most beautiful bedroom I've ever seen. "I hope you'll be comfortable here." Before me, a canopy bed in dark wood with a pale peach silk comforter, wallpaper with flowering vines, and a crystal bowl of white peonies—fresh and perfect—on a table by a window. I stand frozen in the middle of the room, not daring to touch anything. "Your bathroom is right through here," Margaret's saying.

"Thank you," I whisper, unable to say more. Again, I hear my mother's voice. *You'll never belong with these people.*

I push the voice away. They want me here. They invited me.

The Broadmans leave me time to rest and freshen up, after which servers bring out a lunch of hamburgers and grilled chicken sandwiches, potato salad, green salad, and brownies—simple food but perfectly made. I swoon over my brownie and want to hide an extra one in a napkin for later consumption, but don't dare.

The large house is packed with Broadman children, grandchildren, and in-laws; it comes to twenty-three people, I calculate.

"There are twelve bedrooms," Jeremy admits to me, and I soon learn that this is just one of the Broadman homes. I go with it, saying little, observing, and listening to everything. I've accepted the fact that I'm on a new planet that has nothing to do with the one where I grew up and where I'll spend the rest of my life.

It makes me happy to hear from Jeremy that, one by one, some of the younger Broadmans have spoken up on his behalf: first, his little brother Phillip and then his cousin Caroline, who have openly congratulated him for his courage.

But neither Edward and Margaret, nor Jeremy's parents, have said a word about it.

• • •

I don't get a chance to talk to Jeremy, as there are always activities and other people around. We all go to bed early that evening, to rest before the party the next day. It turns out that the event tomorrow, supposedly for family and special friends, will host a hundred people. It'll be an outdoor party, casual, people arriving in short-sleeved shirts and tennis shoes, in some cases bringing tennis rackets or swim clothes.

Among the many graying heads, Jeremy reminds me, is Edward's old Princeton friend, who'll counsel me on my career. "His name's Christopher Byers," Jeremy says. "If we don't find him on our own, Gramps will introduce him to you at lunch."

"Okay." Career counseling, hah. I wonder if Princeton has a degree program for castaways stranded on remote islands. I feel like a party crasher, a street person who has stumbled into a fancy event by mistake and now can't find the exit.

The younger guests seem to have banded together near the pool and tennis courts, as well as a volleyball net that's been set up a distance away on a paved area.

Something familiar. Zack and I used to play two-on-two beach volleyball with some of the guys we knew.

"You wanna play?" I ask Jeremy, nodding in the direction of the net.

"God no. You go ahead, and I'll meet you in an hour."

I jog over there to find a weird mix of players taking their positions. Two buff-looking guys are going to take on five opponents with love-handles and potbellies. The battle lines have been clearly drawn between Flab and Fab.

As I walk up, I again feel out of place, not sure if or where I'll be wanted. I'm hoping the Fabs will recruit me, but don't know if I'm good enough to play on their side. It turns out to be easy. A sixth person joins the Flab team, meaning the Fabs have no choice but to take me.

My two teammates are a tall boy about fourteen, who I immediately name Fab One—or One—and a second guy who gets the name Two.

Two stands across the court, with his back toward me, wearing an olive green t-shirt and black gym shorts. His hair's dark, the color of espresso. He wears it shaggy, not like he intends it to be long, but more like he's been too busy to get it cut. It curls on his neck in a cute way that makes me hope he'll turn around.

Then, someone yells to start the game, and he does—turn around, that is. He has these super-dark eyes, the same espresso color as his hair. The kind that you can tell crinkle in the corners when he smiles.

Wow. In that split second, all my bones disintegrate. I can't move or even take a step, because my body's gone floppy, like a Raggedy Ann doll.

A smile slants across the sexy dark shadow on the lower half of his face. I was right. His eyes do crinkle.

Two walks over to me, while my heart slow dances to meet him. "You play much?" he asks.

"Me? A little." My voice comes out strangely high and breathy. I was pretty good when I played with Zack, but I had bones then.

"Okay, let's roll!" Two's serve rockets over the net to a guy who hits it straight out of bounds.

"One to nothing!"

Two serves again, then again. The Flabs botch both returns, making it seem that even the six to three player ratio is not going to make this game equal. I'm just glad I've gotten a few minutes to pull myself together.

"C'mon, folks! Let's get going." After a minute, the fourteen-year old One, with nothing to do but watch, quits in disgust.

Two and I stand alone on our side. "What do you think?" he asks. "Can we do this?"

"You bet!" The pressure's on now. I need to deliver some Awesome Volleyball.

The six Flabs rally, and we find ourselves challenged. They hit a serve that floats over the net then drops like a stone. With a lunge, Two saves it, sending the ball spinning low in my direction. I somehow get under it and pop it up to where he can get it over the net. "Way to go!" he says, but the ball's coming back at us now.

I tune out everything except for this guy, me, and the game. We call instructions to each other.

"Your ball!" I step back to let him take it.

"Got it!" Two gives me a quick grin as it leaves his fingertips, taking a straight upward vertical path.

I leap high to meet it in mid-air for a spike. *Thwack!* My hand hits the ball over with a satisfying sting.

My muscles coil and uncoil as I move. I can hear Two's breath and the squeak of his shoes on the pavement.

"Watch out!" Going after a ball full-speed, Two almost crashes into me, but leaps sideways to avoid knocking me over, loses his balance, and falls hard.

"Oh!" The onlookers groan as he hits the pavement, but he springs to his feet, ignoring a bloodied elbow, and comes to me. "Are you all right?"

"I'm fine," I say, going warm at the feeling of his hand on my back. He's so beautiful, but older than me, probably in his early twenties.

We are hot and flushed from playing in the sun. My face is probably all red. I bet my hair's awful.

I've just made a really good save.

"Alex!" It's the horrible Emma Broadman. "Great job!" She gives me a thumbs-up from the sidelines, where she stands in a little skirt and sandals.

"Thanks." Since she's barely spoken to me up to now, I wonder why she's suddenly being nice. That is, until I see her run her eyes over Two. And the game's about to end. No wonder she's surfaced right now, like a virus.

After the game, he'll go away. I'll never see him again. A little part of me goes into mourning.

Two sends over a last serve, which the Flabs fumble. The game's over. I'm not sure who won, and I don't care. He comes over to me with a high five, then says, "Your name's Alex?"

"Yeah."

"Are you Alex Marshall?"

"That's me." Not only has this sizzling-hot boy dropped into my life from the sky, but he knows who I am.

He gives a short laugh and says, half to himself, "I thought Alex Marshall was a guy!"

Moving in on us, Emma tries to join the conversation. "I'm glad no one ever thought *I* was a guy!"

Two looks straight at me. "Trust me. I know you're a girl." His eyes glint and the corners of his mouth turn up as he stands there, his hair rumpled, looking adorable. I try to act cool and calm while my knees turn to jelly.

"Will you excuse us?" he says to Emma. "I need to talk to Alex." As her mouth gapes open large enough to spike a volleyball into it, he starts off, motioning me to come with him. We walk across the grass, through an opening in a hedge, and onto one of the walking paths that crisscross the property, which I've learned has fourteen acres.

"How did you know my name?"

"I was asked here to talk to an Alex Marshall. But I assumed it was a guy. Then I heard that girl call you *Alex*."

"What are you supposed to talk to me about?"

"I have no idea."

"Who *are* you?"

He sticks out his right hand. "My name's Christopher Byers."

Chapter Thirty

"*You're* Christopher Byers? I thought you were old!"

"I'm twenty one, if that seems old to you." We walk down the path, away from the crowded party. Trees hang low above us, giving us welcome shade after all our exercise.

Something occurs to me. "Are you a career counselor?"

He laughs at that one. "No. I'm a college student. I'm starting my senior year."

"Then you're here to tell me about Princeton."

"I don't go to Princeton."

I'm out of ideas.

"My grandfather went to Princeton," he says. "He's an old college friend of Edward Broadman's. His name's Christopher Byers, too. Although I go by Chris."

We come to a bench and sit down on it in the shade. Chris leans forward on the bench, his elbows on his knees. I stare at his arms, committing them to memory. On one wrist, he wears a leather string with a seashell on it.

"All I know," Chris says, "is that when Edward Broadman invited my grandfather to the party, he asked if I would come too, as a special favor to him, and talk to a person named Alex Marshall."

"But *why*?"

"I don't know. I was out of the country, about to go home, and got a text that said come here instead."

We stare at each other, mystified. Finally, I ask, "So, if it's not Princeton, where *do* you go to school?"

"Stanford, but this last year, I was mainly down in Monterey, or traveling."

"Why Monterey?"

"I was at The Hopkins Marine Institute. It's part of Stanford. Most people aren't that interested in hearing about it." He runs his hand through his hair, giving me an apologetic look from the side of his eye. "It's where all the marine biology nerds hang out."

He doesn't seem to notice that I've stopped breathing. "Where were you traveling?"

"American Samoa, in the South Pacific. I was just there, doing research on coral with a scientific diving team. But as I say, you're probably not interested in hearing about it."

Pings of excitement run through me. *Thank you, Edward Broadman.* I feel a warm rush of joy and recognition, followed by a creeping fear. Do I really want to know about this wonderful, perfect thing I may never be able to do?

Chris looks at me expectantly, so I take a leap of faith.

"Actually, I'm *very* interested in hearing about it."

• • •

Chris Byers talks for an hour, while I pump him for information. I want to know everything about the diving in Monterey and the Samoas, what kind of work they were doing, how it was to live at the Marine station. He pulls out his cell phone and shows me a picture of himself in a kayak in a lagoon in the South Pacific. "It was the last one taken before the phone ran out of juice, and I couldn't use it again for seven weeks."

He goes on, talking about his future plans. "I'm finishing a double major in biology and environmental science. Then I'll continue at Stanford for my Ph.D. I don't know what my thesis topic will be yet, but something to try to help save the oceans." His dark eyes are serious for a moment, and then twinkle at me again. "*And* something that requires years of field research in beautiful places."

Longing fills me. I can see myself kayaking in a distant lagoon, tagging corals as I fight to find warm-water strains that will thrive and repopulate the world's dying coral reefs. Or better still, it's a kayak for two, and Chris and I are saving the planet together.

Who am I kidding though? This program's for the privileged, not for kids who have to put themselves through school. I refuse to go into debt. Unless I can get full scholarships, I'll work at a dive shop somewhere and go to college at night part-time. Just thinking of that path, compared to what Chris Byers does, is like swallowing the bitterest pill.

"Alex!" I hear my name being shouted from a distance, then Jeremy's little brother Phillip plunges down the path toward us. "Alex!" he exclaims. "We've been looking for you everywhere! Lunch starts in ten minutes."

• • •

Chris and I stop quickly at the house to change clothes, and then head for the huge canopy tent where lunch is being served. The guests sit at round tables with blue and white gingham tablecloths and sunflower centerpieces.

I shake my hands out a little to try to relax. This guy, this future. Everything I want is right here in front of me, yet out of reach.

When we enter the tent, the first person I see is Edward. He stands with a white-haired man in a navy shirt. "Alexandra! I see you found young Chris here. Has he told you about his studies at the Marine Institute?"

"Yes, it's been very interesting." In more ways than one.

"And this is the senior Christopher Byers."

I step forward to shake his hand.

"Hey, Grampa!" Chris and the older man clasp each other's arms, grinning.

"This young lady would make you an excellent diving partner," Edward says to Chris. "She saved my life one day down in a patch of kelp off of Santa Rita Island."

"I heard that story. That was *you?*" Chris's eyes warm with admiration.

"Jeremy's waiting for you at a table, so we'll leave you." Edward and his friend move on, as I spot Jeremy waving at me. "Would you like to sit with us?" I ask Chris, suddenly feeling shy.

It figures that the Broadmans are having a sit-down luncheon for a hundred people at what they have described as a "casual birthday celebration." I slip into a chair next to Jeremy. "I found him," I tell Jeremy, indicating Chris sitting down on my other side. "Christopher Byers."

"I thought you were old," Jeremy tells Chris.

"Yeah, well, *I* thought Alex was a guy."

The two grin at each other.

Chris is now in a dark gray t-shirt and cargo shorts, his bare feet slid into loafers. He's dressed exactly right.

Platters come along offering different choices. One waiter's serving ribs and corn on the cob to what seem to be mainly the younger guests. Given the option of being cute for my new friend or picking ribs and corn out of my teeth while he watches, my choice is clear. I opt for a cold salmon salad, giving the ribs a sad look as they're carried away.

"Why didn't you tell me you were this great diver?" Chris asks, while I admire his straight, perfect eyebrows.

"I guess I didn't think of it."

"I can't believe you're the one who saved Edward Broadman's life! So tell me the story."

I do. "I grew up on Santa Rita Island," I tell him. "I've lived there my whole life."

"What's the diving like down there?"

For the tiniest moment, Zack comes into my head— Zack, who was my friend and diving partner for so many years. Under

211

water, we were the best possible partners— always there for each other. But, on dry land, Zack and I weren't meant to be.

With Chris, though, it feels different. Something's growing in me, a warmth, a certainty. I wonder if he feels it, too.

"I've never been diving anywhere else," I tell him. "But I think Santa Rita's fantastic."

"I should go out there sometime," he says.

"You should."

"And what do you do when you're not diving?"

"School. And I help my mom with her business. She makes wedding cakes."

"Wedding cakes!" To my astonishment, Chris looks interested. "How do you keep one of those things together anyway?"

"Dowel sticks. And cardboard. Large amounts of both." I can't hide my lack of enthusiasm.

"And people eat that?"

"Well, you eat around the dowel sticks and cardboard."

Chris gulps. "Sounds nasty."

"You got that right." I glance over to check on Jeremy. He's telling a story to the people across from him.

Chris's hands are beautiful, tanned and strong. One of them has a long pink welt. I know instantly what it is.

"Ouch," I say in sympathy, pointing to the sting mark.

He looks down. "Yeah," he says. "Jellyfish. Got me in a couple of places."

We sit in silence, while the lunch conversation swirls around us. Something in my life is shifting, tilting in a new direction. I feel it, and I just hope he does, too.

Chris reaches out and touches a strand of hair that's fallen from my ponytail.

"Do you ever wear it down—your hair?" The simple question makes me catch my breath.

"Sometimes," I say. And, although I don't let it show, that's when I feel myself come undone. I'm lost. I'm falling madly and totally in love for the first time in my life.

"Where do you go to school?" He leans forward, toward me, focusing on me as if I'm the only person left on earth.

"Paradise High School." I cringe a little as I say it.

"*High school?*" I could swear all the color has drained from his face.

"But I'll be eighteen in two weeks!"

"You're only seventeen!" He pulls away from me and changes the subject. "So, do you think … you might apply to Stanford next year?"

I come back to reality—hard. "No. I can't." I sit there, biting my lips.

"Financial aid?" he says, hopefully.

"So I can go a quarter million dollars into debt? I don't think so." Not to mention I have to get my last year of high school worked out before I can even start thinking about college.

"Look," Chris says, as if he read my mind. "My dad says there's always a way. You can solve any problem if you work at it."

"You think?" I'm studying his face—the serious dark eyes, his straight nose, the gorgeous dark shadow across his cheeks. I wish I were alone with him, instead of sitting in this crowded place amidst a bazillion senior citizens.

"Yeah," he says, "you can make it happen somehow."

There's a clinking of silverware against glasses, after which Jeremy's Uncle William starts off a round of birthday toasts to Edward. Toasts are clearly big in the Broadman world. I listen as one person after the other offers stories, memories, and congratulations, while the audience laughs and raises champagne glasses.

Jeremy, on my right, sits looking down, pushing his apple pie around its plate with his fork. Guilt hits me. I've talked to Chris through all of lunch.

"You okay?" I ask Jeremy in a low voice.

He shrugs.

"What's wrong?"

"Maybe it's just everything that's been happening. You know, with me and my family."

I wait.

"I've been in a weird mood lately. Doing crazy stuff, you know—like going to Santa Rita for the summer and coming out. I wanna bust loose, do something different."

This is my opening to talk to Jeremy. I smirk at him.

"What?" Jeremy asks, a smile starting on his face. When I don't answer right away, he puts his head close to mine. "C'mon. Spill."

"I've had a brilliant idea." I whisper the details in his ear and then give Jeremy a meaningful look. "So?"

"You're a genius."

"You think?"

"I'm in."

I can't believe it. Jeremy and I sit there, grinning at each other. There's a light touch on my shoulder.

"You guys want to go swimming?" Chris asks.

We answer together. "Yes!"

Chapter Thirty-One

The next morning, before the family brunch begins, Jeremy sidles up to me. "T-7 hours and counting. Authorizations have been secured," he reports gleefully into my ear. "Preparations are in final completion stage."

"Really?" It's unbelievable.

"I'm gonna sit with my folks at breakfast, okay?" he says.

"Fine." I have plans of my own. For this final brunch of family and closest friends, I've broken out my prettiest sundress, put on just a smidge of smoky eyeliner and lip gloss, and brushed my hair until it falls across my shoulders in glossy, voluptuous waves. I hope Chris will notice.

He gets a funny look on his face when he sees me. "You look great," is all he says, but it's enough. He doesn't leave my side for the rest of the morning.

He sits across from me, eating a waffle. Every move he makes enchants me. The way he drinks his juice is cute. The way he eats his egg is sexy. I wish I could be the strawberry on his plate.

I can't see Jeremy, as he's down the table from me, on my side, but I hear his voice in brief snatches. Chris and I are quiet through the whole meal, letting the others carry the conversation. All I can think of is escaping, to be alone with him for even a few minutes before we each take off in our different directions.

But it is not to be. As the meal ends, Chris's grandfather stands. "This has been delightful," he announces, "but we have a plane to catch." They're heading for the Bay Area, where they live and where Chris will return to school.

Luther's going to drive them to the airport, then come back to take me to the Traveler terminal a few hours later. As the others walk ahead, Chris slows down and pulls me to the side. He hands me his cell phone. "Will you give me yours?"

We stand close together, each entering our numbers into the other's phones, after which he slips his into the front pocket of his shirt. He takes a deep breath and faces me.

"So," he says, "this is it."

"Bye." I've just barely met him and now have to say goodbye. My eyes sting. He won't call me. I'll never see him again.

I walk him out to the car and watch as he gets in, looking back at me for a quick moment and tapping the front shirt pocket that holds his phone with my numbers, as if to say *I won't forget.* The door closes, the limo slides away, and Chris vanishes.

• • •

"Alex, may I speak to you before you leave?" Edward waves me into the library, which has entire walls filled with books, richly colored rugs and several seating areas in soft leather furniture.

I feel almost light-headed as I sit down, thrilled about my scheme with Jeremy, yet so sad that Chris is gone from my life, probably forever. I touch the dark brown leather of my chair, amazed by its softness. I'll never get used to the way these people live.

Margaret comes in and sits in a chair beside me. "I wanted to be here, too," she says.

"We just have a few minutes now, but please be sure, when you apply to colleges next year, to give me your list of schools," Edward says. "I plan to write personal letters of recommendation on your behalf to each Dean of Admissions."

"Thank you!" I look up at him, finding it hard to believe that this powerful man once needed me, would have died without my help. And now he wants to help me.

"Furthermore, Alex, my assistant Ruth will be calling you. I'm on the board of several private scholarship foundations, and she'll be sending you information on how to apply, if you would like to."

I nod as my heart starts to pound.

"The scholarships are based on merit, and I'm just one vote on the committee, but still, I would urge you to apply. The foundations are well funded and help a number of deserving students every year."

"I'd love to apply! Thank you for the opportunity. And for this weekend. I had such a good time."

Margaret gives me a sweet, warm smile. "Alexandra, I cannot express enough what you've done for us. I hope you know that, on the day you saved Edward's life, you became a member of our family."

I can barely speak. "I never had grandparents," I blurt, then flush with embarrassment. What a dumb thing to say.

Margaret doesn't seem to feel that way. "Well now you do," she says with a sharp nod of her head.

There's something I want them to know. "Did Jeremy ever tell you the story of when he and I went out on the dive boat?"

They shake their heads.

"He saved my life that day." And I describe what happened. How Jeremy had shared his air with me and stayed with me, even when his own life was at risk. How he and I had brought Tom up to the surface together. When I finish, Margaret's chin is trembling.

"That dear boy," she says.

"He *is*," I say. "He's my best friend in the whole world."

Edward clears his throat, his voice gruff. "We didn't know this. Thank you, Alex, for telling us."

We hear a knock. Luther is at the door of the study. "I'll be needing to get Miss Alex on her way, sir." He touches the brim of his cap as he addresses Edward and picks up my overnight bag to carry it down.

Jeremy waits for us at the bottom of the steps by the limo. He and I give each other excited grins.

"Where's your stuff?" I ask him.

"Already in the trunk." He's practically bursting open with anticipation. He puts me in the back seat, while Luther adds my bag in beside his. "I'll be right back." He goes up the front steps two at a time and envelopes Edward and Margaret in giant hugs, then runs back down. He piles into the back of the limo, while Luther gets into the driver's seat.

Luther's eyebrows lift in surprise."Mr. Jeremy, you're riding with us? No one told me."

"Last minute decision," Jeremy says.

Luther pauses, then asks delicately, "You be making the round trip with me?"

"Nope," Jeremy says, looking enormously pleased with himself. "One way."

• • •

When Jeremy and I explain our plans for the school year to Mom and Lester, they stare at us in amazement. Mom and I have a week left together in the house, during which time Lester will be at the Channel Island Resort, where Jessica's getting married next Saturday. Jeremy will be camped with his suitcases up at the Inn.

"Jeremy, I thought you were going to college!" Mom says.

"I'll go next September, but I decided to take a gap year first." He gives me one of his evil looks. "It was all Alex's idea."

Mom and Lester exchange glances over that piece of information.

"But what will you do here all winter?" Mom asks.

218

"Work full-time for Dizzy. I want to learn the restaurant business."

"What about housing?" Lester asks now with a cautious expression on his face.

There's a silence, which I finally break. "We're going to be roommates. Here. We'll take over Mom's lease."

Mom turns purple. *"Roommates!"*

"It's completely appropriate," Jeremy reassures her. "I'm not wired for women."

Lester chokes slightly, but absorbs this news in silence. Their mouths are opening and closing like two goldfish.

"Alex, the house was rented out. Just yesterday." Mom' voice is laced with relief, as if she's thinking *Way to kill this idea!*

Rented out. It's like getting a swift, hard uppercut, perfectly placed for maximum damage to my body organs. I sink down into an armchair. "We'll find someplace else," I say, hardly daring to look at Jeremy. I can't believe it. He deferred Stanford for a year, and now we don't have a place to live.

"No worries," Jeremy says.

"The owner just rented our house out from under our noses! To some, some *dirtbag!*" I'm completely freaking out. "How can you say *no worries?*"

Jeremy is unruffled. "Because she rented it to me."

He breaks the stunned silence. "When you told me yesterday the owner had it listed for rent, I knew we had to move fast. So I called her and snapped the place up." He clears his throat. "I meant to tell you."

"You really *are* a Broadman," I tell him, full of admiration.

Mom is having none of it. "Alex, you can't afford to pay half this rent. You don't even know what you're doing."

"Yes, I do."

"How do you plan to meet your expenses?"

"She doesn't have to meet any expenses," Jeremy interrupts.

"Oh, yes, I do," I tell him. "We're going Dutch, or you're going home!"

"But how, Alex?" Mom insists.

I make her wait for a long moment before I say the words in my head.

"I'm going to make wedding cakes."

Chapter Thirty-Two

I could work at Nate's Dive Shop for a salary, but my number crunching has shown me that, if I order wholesale and raise my prices, I can make much better money from my own wedding cake business. Winter's a slow time on the island for weddings, with maybe only five or six a month, but that's fine with me. I just need to cover my half of the rent, plus food and utilities.

"Evelyn?" She's the first person I call.

"Alex! I was at my wit's end! We have two weddings booked here at the Inn for October and no way to get a cake!" We both know no wedding cake would ever survive a boat trip across the channel.

"Well, I'm here and in business," I tell her. "I'm doing it part time this year, while I finish high school."

Evelyn seems to hesitate. "I probably shouldn't say this."

I wait.

"You *must* take my advice. With your mom going away, you're the only person on the island who can make a decent wedding cake. *Price accordingly.*"

"You think?" It's a relief to hear Evelyn, who's so experienced, confirm that I'm on the right track.

"Alex, I've watched you work your fingers to the bone for your mother for more years than I care to count. Now I'm telling you. Raise your prices at least two dollars a slice. You'll still be very competitive, but you'll make some real money, and have time for a little fun, for once, your last year of high school."

"Thanks, Evelyn. I will."

"*And* I'll give you all the Inn's business."

I swallow hard. "You know I can't do the really fancy cakes," I warn her.

"I don't think there's anything you can't do, Alex. Besides, I've seen your cakes, and they're lovely."

I can't believe how lucky I am, how wonderful my life is. "How's Rebecca doing?" I ask.

"Great! She's got a regular gig at Sam's Joint playing Tuesday nights. She's over the moon about it."

"I'll go see her for sure," I say.

• • •

Jessica Lindstrom is married the following Saturday in her grandmother's heirloom diamond necklace and a floor-length gown that looks like spun sugar. She carries a bouquet of white orchids, the same ones that are on the dinner tables.

Mom goes crazy over the wedding cake, which must be a thousand percent perfect for Lester's daughter. She and Lester decorate it together with more of his home-grown white orchids, and it is, in fact, perfect—exactly what Jessica had dreamed of.

Mom attends as Lester's fiancee, and I'm there, too, in my new status as Jessica's future stepsister. I wear my hand-me-down green silk dress and Jeremy comes as my plus one, looking handsome in a dark suit.

As she and her new husband prepare to leave for their Hawaiian honeymoon, Jessica tosses her bouquet of white orchids in a high arc heading straight for me. I sidestep to let the bridesmaid beside me stretch for it, snagging it with a triumphant cry. "Way to go!"

I tell her. I won't need a wedding of my own anytime soon. One day, when I'm ready, there'll be another bouquet for me to catch.

• • •

Jeremy, my mom, and I stand at the Traveler boat terminal. Lester went back Monday and will meet Mom's boat this afternoon in Long Beach.

I wonder what strange upside-down world I've wandered into, where Jeremy and I are staying on the island together, while my mother, of all people, is leaving for the mainland to begin a new life. I would never have predicted it, but, again, it's perfect.

I'm so sorry to miss your birthday," she says for the hundredth time. "But this Lindstrom family reunion…"

"It's really okay, Mom. We've already celebrated."

"Alex, you're a good girl. I probably haven't said it as often as I should. But I'm so proud of you! I love you."

"Me, too." We hug each other hard.

"Give Lester my love." I say it automatically, without even thinking. And I mean it.

Jeremy and I wave until Mom has disappeared into the boat. I give a shaky sigh. "There she goes. My only family in the whole world."

"Really?" Jeremy asks. "You don't have cousins or uncles or something?"

"Nope."

Jeremy puts an arm around my shoulder. "I'll be your family."

"*Will you?*"

"Sure. And Gram and Gramps, too. Sometimes, you gotta go out and choose your own family. Or let them choose you."

"I guess you're right." In addition to Mom, I have Jeremy. And Edward and Margaret. And Jenna and Dizzy. And Zack. They aren't family in the normal sense of the word, but they love me and I can count on them.

Then there's Lester. I've always thought of him as belonging to Mom, but a new idea has been rolling through my head since Jessica's wedding. Lester's going to be my stepfather. Which is kind of like being my father. I try it on for size, the idea of Lester as my dad. I can live with it. Easily.

Funny that I haven't noticed until now how crisp and cool the air is and how sharply the Santa Rita mountains stand out against the sky. The masts of the sailboats tilt back and forth in the harbor, while seagulls circle.

I link arms with Jeremy. "Did you call home today?" I ask as we start off.

"Yeah, I did." Jeremy's parents still treat him coolly, but Edward and Margaret have officially thrown in their support, so he has hope for the future. He's taken over my mom's old bedroom, plastering on its door a bumper sticker from the Dizzy box. It reads: *The truth shall set you free.*

School has started. I'm broke, as usual, but it doesn't matter, because I have a skill that will allow me to pay my own way. I know how to make wedding cakes.

I'm on my own, independent, and rooming with my best friend. My life is fantastic. Except for one thing.

Chris and I haven't spoken. At all.

Neither of us has called the other, and in my case, I know why. I came home from the Broadmans thinking, *what am I doing?* I've just met this guy. At the Broadmans' house, I'd liked him so much. But now that I can't see him or hear his voice anymore, he feels like a stranger again.

Maybe he feels the same way. And he thought I was young.

That night I go by Jenna and Dizzy's house. Jenna's starting to show a little and blooms with happiness. They're converting their second bedroom office into a nursery.

I find myself telling them about Chris. Remembering our recent conversation, I ask, "You guys? How old were you when you first met?

224

"Well, let's see,"Jenna replies. "I was eighteen and Dizzy was twenty-two."

"Chris seemed freaked out that I was only seventeen."

"Good!" Dizzy booms.

"He couldn't believe I was still in high school."

"In even a few years, it won't matter, but I can see how it might feel to him, right now," Dizzy says. "A senior in college dating a high school girl? It's like, hey, can't you get a girl your own age?"

"Was the age difference a problem for you?"

"Not really," Dizzy says. He comes up behind Jenna and puts his arms around her waist, patting her belly. "When something's meant to be, you don't fight it."

He's right.

"I have to go home," I say. "I have a phone call to make."

• • •

Jeremy's working a shift at Dizzy's, so I have the house to myself. I take out my cell phone and find Chris's number, then pace around my bedroom, listening to his phone ring.

"Hello—Alex?"

I almost trip over my own feet. "Hi!"

"I saw your name on the display screen. I'm glad you called." His voice starts out warm and happy, but turns embarrassed. "I kept starting to call you, then hanging up."

"If you wanted to call me, why didn't you?"

"Alex," he says. "I can't do this. You're in high school."

"I'm turning eighteen this weekend. Anyway, I'm not ready right now for … for anything really intense."

"We could just be friends," he says.

"Okay." Even as I say it, I wonder how long that will last.

After a moment he says, "So, your birthday's this weekend? Big plans?"

"Not really." I tell him about Mom and Lester and about living with Jeremy. "You should come down sometime. Dive Santa Rita."

225

"I'd like that." I can feel him hesitating on the other end. "I'm not sure when, though. I'm starting a project that's gonna have me tied up on a lot of weekends this fall."

"Oh." I feel a pang of disappointment, even though twenty minutes ago I'd been resigned to never seeing him ever again. "When does your project start?"

"End of September." He lets a few seconds pass. "I'm free this weekend, though."

"This weekend?" I repeat, stupidly.

"Yeah. If you want, I could come down for your birthday."

I'm thinking fast. It would just be me, Chris, and Jeremy in the house. "Do you mind sleeping on our sofa?"

"No."

"Well, then, that would be nice. If you came, I mean."

This is great.

This is terrifying.

I'll see Chris again in three days.

• • •

At twelve noon on the day of my eighteenth birthday, I find myself waiting for the Traveler as I fidget and twirl a piece of my hair. The boat's late. I pick at a fingernail.

I'm dying to see him.

I'm scared to see him.

Also waiting to meet the boat are Annabelle and Trish. I wave to them, thinking, *terrific, an audience*. I hope they collect their people and leave before Chris appears.

No such luck. He's one of the first off the boat. He wears jeans and a plaid flannel shirt, and he carries a heavy dive bag in one hand. In the other arm he's carrying—*omigod*—this sheaf of pale yellow roses wrapped in cellophane and ribbon. They're just past the bud stage, fresh and lovely, and he stands there holding them out to me with the warmest look in his eyes, while I melt away into a whiff of vapor.

226

"Eighteen roses for your eighteenth birthday."

I somehow manage to take them and greet him normally, kissing him on his freshly shaven cheek that smells of pine. I could easily stay there for a while, even take up residence with my face against his cheek, but I tear myself away.

Trish and Annabelle openly ogle us. *Go ahead,* I think to myself. He's even more gorgeous than I remembered. As always and without my intending it, the island will be talking about me.

I put Chris in my wedding cake van and take him home to Cinnamon Street. As we walk in, I have a feeling of unreality. The dirty, crumbling little house, where I grew up trapped under my mother's thumb has completely changed. It's clean and tidy, and in the short time that Jeremy and I have lived together, we've bought plants, put colorful throws over the old sofa and armchair, and hung posters on the walls. Today there are bunches of balloons that Jeremy supplied for my birthday. I place Chris's roses in a vase on the coffee table, where they dominate the room.

For the first time in my life, my house looks like a home. And it feels like a home, too. Yesterday, Jeremy announced that he's going to make me a birthday dinner.

"But you can't cook!" I said.

"I can read. And I have a recipe."

Jenna and Dizzy will be coming tonight to celebrate with us as well as Evelyn and Rebecca, who has promised to bring her guitar. Even Zack and Rosie are going to drop by.

Before the party, though, I have afternoon plans for me and Chris. "We're going diving," I tell him. I hadn't realized how excited I would be to show Chris my island. He's been to some of the most beautiful places in the world. But he's never seen the giant sea bass of Santa Rita, and I'm counting on them to make a good impression.

I take him to Squatter's Cove in one of Kap's little skiffs. By now, it's late afternoon, and the water has a pearly iridescent sheen to it.

'You're going to meet the Hulk," I tell Chris. "If we can find him."

We let our anchor down and pull on our gear, taking care not to tip the small boat. But I make the mistake of balancing my fins on the seat by the edge of the boat. The next thing I know, one of them's in the water.

"Got it!" Chris scoops the fin up before it can sink. Instead of giving it to me, he picks up my foot and slips the fin onto it. He puts the second fin on my other foot. "At your service," he says, grinning, his hand on my ankle.

My heart pounds like a jackhammer. "You ready to go?" I try to make my voice sound normal. Here in Squatter's Cove, Zack and I have dived and seen the Hulk so many times. It feels new and strange to have Chris as a partner, but I'm ready for the change.

We descend. The water's more than a hundred feet deep here, so the kelp plants are enormous and eerie, rooted in the ocean floor and twisting their way up through the water. It has the feeling of a holy place, with the kelp rising like the spires of a cathedral, its leaves rippling. I can sense Chris beside me, taking it in, savoring the weird beauty of the kelp forest.

We start to explore.

Chris points. My eyes follow his hand over to a couple of large bat rays. Flat creatures with billowing wings and long tails, they move like ghosts through the water. A few moments later, we pass over a ledge where a sand-colored angel shark lies camouflaged, waiting for his dinner to swim by. Luckily, humans aren't usually on the menu. We circle over it for a minute, then move on.

We're at a depth of only thirty feet when we spot the sea bass, three of them, suspended in the kelp. They hover in front of us like misshapen black blimps.

It's the enormous Hulk and his bodyguards. Even the two smaller ones are several times my size, weighing in at over four hundred pounds. Slow swimming and very curious, they're known as the "gentle giants."

The immense fish approach. As we remain still, I can feel Chris radiating excitement next to me, the same that I'm feeling. The Hulk, who's probably six feet long, stops, his whiskery lips opening and closing within inches of our masks as we exchange a silent greeting. He passes between us, seeming to go on forever as he drifts by. Another passes above us and a third in front of us, close enough to touch.

For a moment, Chris and I stay motionless, stunned by the experience. Joy wells up in me as we slowly ascend, our heads breaking the water close to the boat.

We pull ourselves aboard. "That was amazing," Chris says.

I'm proud of my little island for holding its own against all the spectacular places where Chris has dived. Even though I'll leave this island, *need* to leave it, it will always be my home.

It grows late. While we inch off our wetsuits, I think how lucky I am to be a diver, and therefore destined to spend time with guys in bathing suits. Chris's body in a Speedo is like the eighth natural wonder of the world. I do a quick check to make sure all the parts to my bikini are still guarding their appointed posts.

Neither of us speak, not wanting to break the spell of the afternoon. We're alone in a small boat, wearing nothing but skimpy bathing suits. The air cools as evening comes. Chris grabs our sweatshirts, which we put on.

"It's funny. When we're apart, all I can think about is that you're in high school." His eyes take in my face, my wet hair curling in all directions. "But when I'm with you, it doesn't seem to matter."

Conflicting thoughts race through my head. I've just met him. He's special. He's in college. I don't care.

Just being near him sets my body on fire. "But nothing's going to happen," I think, and then realize I've said it out loud.

"Something already *has* happened," he says. "At least, for me." His eyes are so vulnerable that I take his hand.

"For me, too."

Chris looks at me like I'm the only person in the world, like there's nothing he could possibly want to do more than be with me.

It's all starting to come together for me. Chris, this year on the island with Jeremy. Sue's marriage to Lester and even Jenna and Dizzy's new baby. And most of all, an open path before me. I still have to prove myself, get admitted to college, earn the scholarships. But I'm free to try. And to go.

It's there in that tiny boat anchored at Squatter's Cove that Chris kisses me for the first time, slowly pulling me in and delivering the sweetest, hottest, most lingering kiss I could ever have imagined. His mouth is gentle, like it's getting to know me, exploring my lips and then traveling down my neck, while a four-alarm fire rages inside my bikini. I cling to him, thinking *Don't ever let me go.* And he doesn't. We kiss for a long time, until he finally says, "It'll be dark soon."

I pull away from him, beginning to surface from my trance and remember the other parts of my life.

"We should go home," I say. "To Jeremy. He's got dinner waiting." And a party to celebrate the best birthday I've ever had.

Chris starts the motor, and we head off, as the sun sends its pink tendrils out across the ocean's surface, falls to the horizon, and disappears from sight.

Also by Anne Pfeffer

Any Other Night

...My head begins to pound, and suddenly, all I can think of is Michael, taking off on his cosmic rocket ride into death. Inside me, I feel a tearing, as if something huge and made of steel—a battleship or a skyscraper—is being pulled apart.

And Emily sees the expression on my face and doesn't ask a bunch of dumb questions about how I feel, but just looks at me, and I say "It's Michael," as the pain rips into me.

She puts her arm around me and squeezes—hard. Her hand, which grips my right shoulder, is surprisingly strong. I can almost feel strength flowing out of her fingers and into my shoulder, straightening my back. I feel myself relax.

"I miss him," I say.

The sympathy in her eyes is like a warm bath.

If girls were flames, most girls would be a single match, a mere Bic lighter. Emily, on the other hand, would be an inferno—a raging, thousand-acre forest fire.

Finalist in the 2012 Indie Reader Discovery Awards competition

56000081R00140

Made in the USA
Charleston, SC
10 May 2016